D0394966

AN
ARAMINTA SPOOKIE
ADVENTURE

Gargoyle
Hall

AN
ARAMINTA SPOOKIE
ADVENTURE

Gargoyle
Hall

ANGIE SAGE

illustrated by
JOHN KELLY

BLOOMSBURY
NEW YORK LONDON OXFORD NEW DELHI SYDNEY

First published in Great Britain in June 2014 by Bloomsbury Publishing Plc
Published in the United States of America in August 2015 by Bloomsbury Children's Books
www.bloomsbury.com

Bloomsbury is a registered trademark of Bloomsbury Publishing Plc

For information about permission to reproduce selections from this book, write to
Permissions, Bloomsbury Children's Books, 1385 Broadway, New York, New York 10018
Bloomsbury books may be purchased for business or promotional use. For information on bulk
purchases please contact Macmillan Corporate and Premium Sales Department at
specialmarkets@macmillan.com

Library of Congress Cataloging-in-Publication Data
Sage, Angie.
Gargoyle Hall : an Araminta Spookie adventure / by Angie Sage ; illustrated by John Kelly.
pages   cm
Summary: When strange moans echo down the halls of her boarding school,
junior detective Araminta is determined to solve the mystery.
ISBN 978-1-61963-626-2 (hardcover) • ISBN 978-1-61963-700-9 (e-book)
[1. Mystery and detective stories. 2. Boarding schools—Fiction. 3. Schools—Fiction.
4. Haunted places—Fiction.] I. Kelly, John, illustrator. II. Title.
PZ7.S13035Gar 2015   [Fic]—dc23   2014028390

Typeset by Dorchester Typesetting Group Ltd
Printed and bound in the U.S.A. by Thomson-Shore Inc., Dexter, Michigan
2 4 6 8 10 9 7 5 3 1

All papers used by Bloomsbury Publishing, Inc., are natural, recyclable products
made from wood grown in well-managed forests. The manufacturing processes
conform to the environmental regulations of the country of origin.

For
Isabella Blount,
with love

CONTENTS

BAT TROUBLE

When I grow up, I want to be a detective and solve Mysteries. To get into training I have set up Spookie's Detective Agency. I am chief detective and my friend Wanda Wizzard is my sidekick. This means Wanda helps out in the detective agency and sometimes goes on Mystery-solving expeditions with me. Well, that is the idea, anyway.

Running a detective agency is not easy, because first you need a Mystery to solve. In films and books, people go to a detective agency and ask them to solve a Mystery. But no one has come to Spookie's Detective Agency and asked it to solve anything yet. I don't know why. So I have to find my own Mysteries to solve. Weeks can go by without any kind of Mystery and then, just like buses, a whole load of Mysteries arrive at once. This is what happened recently. The first to arrive was the Mystery of Uncle Drac's Traveling Sleeping Bag.

It all began after my uncle Drac came back from his vacation to see the giant bats of Transylvania. Suddenly he started acting strangely. Of course, most people would think that Uncle Drac acted strangely *before* he went on vacation. That is probably because Uncle Drac has a turret full of bats, where he sleeps in a flowery sleeping bag, which hangs from the rafters at the very top of the turret. I don't think that many uncles do that. Well, not in a *flowery* sleeping bag, anyway.

Before he went on vacation, Uncle Drac used to spend all day happily sleeping in the bat turret surrounded by his bats. But when he came back from vacation, that changed. He began to hang around the house—and when I say hang around, I mean it literally. One day I found him in his sleeping bag hanging behind the door of the ghost-in-the-bath-bathroom. The next day he was hanging from the balustrades on the top landing, and the day after that, I tripped over him because his sleeping bag had fallen off the coat hooks by the front door. It was very unsettling. I never knew where Uncle Drac would turn up next.

When I told my sidekick about the Mystery of Uncle Drac's Traveling Sleeping Bag, she did not look impressed. She said, "But, Araminta, why don't we just ask Uncle Drac why he isn't sleeping in the bat turret anymore?"

I sighed. "Look, Wanda," I said. "A detective can't go around *asking* people why they are doing mysterious things."

"Why not?" Wanda asked.

"Because people would tell them the answers and then there wouldn't be any Mysteries to solve, would there? So then there wouldn't be any detectives."

But later on, when I found Uncle Drac in his sleeping bag in the boiler room, I decided to take my sidekick's advice and ask him why he was not sleeping in the bat turret anymore.

Uncle Drac groaned when I prodded him awake, and he poked his head up over the top of the sleeping bag. "Wherrrsit, Minty?" he mumbled. Uncle Drac always calls me "Minty," which I really like.

"Uncle Drac, why aren't you sleeping in the bat turret anymore?" I asked.

Uncle Drac groaned and said, "Don't ask, Minty. Just *don't*."

"But I just *did* ask, Uncle Drac," I said.

"I know you did," said Uncle Drac. "And I would rather not say, if you don't mind." Then he slid back down into the sleeping bag. As I was walking out of the boiler room, Uncle Drac popped his head up again. "Minty . . . ," he said.

Aha, I thought. This is what always happens.

As the detective walks away, the suspect has second thoughts and calls her back to confess all. Not that Uncle Drac was a suspect—well, not at that point, anyway.

"Yes, Uncle Drac?" I said nonchalantly. Being *nonchalant* is what you have to do a lot of when you are a detective. It means behaving as if you are not really bothered about something, even if you are. It is a very good way of getting people to tell you things. However, it didn't work this time.

"Do *not* go into the bat turret," Uncle Drac said.

"Oh. Why not, Uncle Drac?" I asked, looking up at the ceiling at some spiderwebs so that it seemed like I was still being nonchalant.

"Because I say so," said Uncle Drac, sounding rather grumpy. "And that goes for Wanda, too."

"All right, Uncle Drac," I said, and I ran off to find my sidekick. I wanted to tell her that we now had another Mystery to solve—the Mystery of the Forbidden Bat Turret.

But even that Mystery did not interest my sidekick. All she said was, "But, Araminta, you *know* we are not allowed in the bat turret. It is dangerous in there."

Wanda does not like the bat turret. This is because Uncle Drac has taken all the floors out to give his bats lots of space to fly around. This means that when you climb in through the little red door at the top of the turret, you look straight down to the very bottom, which is covered with bat poo. Wanda is afraid of falling all the way down, even though I think it would be quite a soft landing, really, as the bat poo is very thick. But Wanda does not like bat poo.

Even though Wanda can be very boring about bats and turrets and bat poo, she is my best friend (most of the time). Wanda lives in Spookie House with me and we share our bedrooms. We have a bedroom for every day of the week, which is fun.

There are other people in Spookie House too: Wanda's mom and dad, Brenda and Barry Wizzard, and also Pusskins, Brenda's smelly old cat (who is not a person, even though Brenda seems to think she is). There is also my uncle Drac, who you have already met. Then there is my aunt Tabby, and you are lucky not to have met her yet, but you will, because no one escapes Aunt Tabby for very long.

The best thing about Spookie House is the ghosts. We have three. We have a ghost in armor called Sir Horace, his faithful hound called Fang, and his weedy page called Edmund.

As I said, once you have one Mystery, lots more start coming along. The next one arrived that evening—it was the Mystery of the Terrified Bats. It all began when I was downstairs in the hall playing with Fang. In Spookie House there is a very big entrance hall. It has a wide flight of stairs with a banister that is really fun to slide down; it has lots of doors that go off into other rooms, a huge clock, some funny old chairs all around the walls, and a lot of weird stuffed animals in cases that Wanda's mom has started collecting. Most of the animals are cats wearing

clothes. They are actually quite creepy, but I always look in the cases because I hope that one day I will see Pusskins in there too. I don't think Aunt Tabby likes the stuffed cats either, because she does not even go near them with her duster, which means there are a lot of lovely spiderwebs all over them.

Fang was running to catch a ball—which he never can because he is a ghost—when the doorbell rang and kept on ringing, because our doorbell gets stuck. Aunt Tabby came scooting out of one of the doors to answer it. She pulled open the front door, banged the doorbell hard to make it stop, and then said, "Oh!" She did not sound pleased. But I soon knew why, because the next thing she said was, "Come in, Emilene. What a surprise."

Bother, I thought. It was Great-aunt Emilene, Uncle Drac's mother. Great-aunt Emilene is scary—even Aunt Tabby is a little bit scared of her. She always wears a long black coat and has a double-ended ferret around her neck. A double-ended ferret is actually two ferrets stitched together to make a kind of creepy ferret-scarf. It means that when you look at Great-aunt Emilene, two dead little ferret faces with glassy eyes stare back at you.

"Are you staying long?" Aunt Tabby asked Great-aunt Emilene.

Great-aunt Emilene sniffed, rather like Wanda does. And then she said, "For as long as it takes, Tabitha."

As long as what takes? I wanted to ask, and I think Aunt Tabby did too. But neither of us said anything.

Great-aunt Emilene strode in and stopped beside me and Fang—who she can't see because she does not believe in ghosts. So all she saw was me rolling the ball and then running to pick it up by myself. "It is very sad," Great-aunt Emilene said to Aunt Tabby.

"What is very sad?" Aunt Tabby asked suspiciously.

"That an excitable child like Araminta should be always playing on her own like this. It will lead to all kinds of trouble, mark my words." And then she swept off toward the big smart room that Aunt Tabby keeps (fairly) clean for guests to go into.

Aunt Tabby did not look pleased. "But she has Wanda to play with," I heard her say as she hurried after my great-aunt.

"Wanda. Huh!" I heard Great-aunt Emilene say with another sniff as the door closed behind them.

I listened at the door a bit but could not hear anything except for Great-aunt Emilene droning on and Aunt Tabby occasionally saying, "No." It got boring after a while, so I decided to build a spider pyramid. One of my hobbies—when I am not busy running the detective agency—is making houses for spiders. Recently I have expanded that to include acrobatics for spiders, because it is good for spiders to do some kind of sport. I found five really good spiders dangling from the stuffed-cat cases and took them upstairs to the landing to make a spider pyramid. Fang came too. He was watching me with his tongue hanging out, and every now and then he tried to snap at one. I don't think Fang understands that he is a ghost and ghosts cannot eat anything, not even spiders.

As I expect you know, it is not easy to make a spider pyramid, because spiders have so many legs and they get tangled up. Also, they keep running away. It seems to me that they do not like making pyramids. I don't know why. If I were a spider I would think that spider pyramids were really fun. Anyway, after trying for ages, all my spiders seemed to have gotten used to the idea of being in a pyramid. But just as I was about to put the last spider on the top, Fang threw back his head and began to howl. Fang has a really great spine-chilling howl but it does not make balancing the top spider on the pyramid very easy.

"**Arrooooh!**" Fang howled. "**Arrooooooooooh!**"

"Shush, Fang," I said. "Just wait a minute until I have finished."

But Fang would not wait. He kept on howling. He was so loud that I am surprised I heard Wanda scream at all. But I did. From somewhere high up in Spookie House, I heard a distinctive Wanda-scream.

"Aaaiiiieeeeee! Help! Gerrrrroffmeeeee!"

Wanda used to scream a lot when she first moved into Spookie House, but now that she is used to all the ghosts and spiders—and to Aunt Tabby—she hardly screams at all. But this scream was just like one of Wanda's early ones. It was very loud and piercing and it made my ears ring. I wondered what she was screaming about

and thought that maybe another Mystery was about to happen. So, because a chief detective is never off duty, I went to find out. Fang came lolloping after me.

We followed Wanda's screams all the way to the top of the house and the little red door that leads into Uncle Drac's bat turret. It was wide open and a long stream of bats was flying out like a black cloud. Fang sat down and howled again and then I remembered—Fang always howls at bats.

The screams were coming from a bat-covered Wanda shape lying on the floor with her hands over her head. "*Aaeeiiiiii!*" she was yelling. "Get them off meeeee! They are stuck in my *hair*!"

It was true—some of the bats *were* stuck in Wanda's hair. Poor bats. Bats have sweet little claws on the end of their wings and their delicate claws had gotten all tangled in Wanda's hair. The bats were flapping their wings like crazy, trying to get away from her. Who can blame them? She was making a horrible noise. Bats don't like loud noises; they have very sensitive hearing, and the ones that were stuck in her hair were panicking because they were really close to where the noise was coming from. It was not, as I pointed out to Wanda, very nice for the bats at all.

"It is not very nice for *me*, either, Araminta!" yelled Wanda. "*Get them off!*"

As I am Wanda's best friend, I decided to do what she asked. There is only one thing to do when someone is covered in bats, and that is what I did—I really don't know why everyone made such a fuss about it afterward. I rushed along to the drowned-nun-in-the-bath-bathroom and was back a few seconds later with a bucket of cold water. I threw the water over Wanda and the bats.

This is something I learned from Uncle Drac—the best way to calm down a panicking bat is to throw cold water at it. Once a bat is covered in cold water it stops making a fuss. Being covered in cold water is not very nice for the bat, but sometimes in an emergency, you have to do it. And I thought this was definitely an emergency.

The cold water worked perfectly. Even though Wanda was still squealing like a little pig, all the bats stuck in her hair went very still and stopped struggling. They sat and dripped and looked really fed up, because bats do not like cold water. The trouble was, neither did Wanda—which was something she had in common with bats (although when I told her that, she did not look impressed). While the bats were still shocked I carefully untangled their delicate little claws from Wanda's hair, and then I put them up on a nearby chest so that they would be out of the way of Aunt Tabby's big feet while they dried out.

Unfortunately, Aunt Tabby's big feet did not stay out of the way of *me*. Suddenly I heard a voice yelling, "Araminta! Araminta, what are you doing *now*?" and Aunt Tabby whizzed around the corner. She skidded to a halt and her eyes went all wide and round like they were going to pop out of her head. Aunt Tabby stared at the empty bucket and the soggy bats and then she stared at Wanda, who had stood up and was dripping like an old tap. Wanda was making a real mess of the rug, which had a big squelchy puddle on it. I could see that Aunt Tabby was not happy about something. I guessed it was the rug but I was wrong.

"Araminta Spookie!" she said. Then she stopped as though she had run out of words. I sighed. I knew it was bad. Aunt Tabby only says my last name when she is extra-specially mad.

"Yes, Aunt Tabby?" I asked in my best angelic way. I am perfecting being angelic as I think it

will come in handy when I am trying to lull sus-pects into what is called a false sense of security.

"You can take that dying duck expression off your face right now," Aunt Tabby told me.

I frowned. I do not think you should make jokes about dying ducks.

"And it is no good looking sulky, either," Aunt Tabby said snappily.

Wanda sniffed noisily and rubbed her nose on the end of her sleeve. It is a disgusting habit of hers, but Aunt Tabby did not even notice. She was too busy asking me stupid questions. Like, "Did you throw this bucket of water over poor Wanda?"

The bucket was actually empty, but I knew it was not the time to be what Uncle Drac calls pedantic. So I went for the angelic expression again and said, "Yes, Aunt Tabby, I did."

"But *why?*" Aunt Tabby wailed.

I sighed and began to explain. "It was a bat emergency. Wasn't it, Wanda?" I thought it was about time Wanda backed me up. After all, she had been yelling for help and I had been really nice and helped her. But Wanda did not back me up. All she did was drip more on the rug and then go, "Achoo . . . Achoo . . . Achoo-achoo-*achoo*!" Wanda always overdoes sneezing. It has to be at least five times.

The sneezes brought Brenda thumping up the stairs. Brenda may not recognize a yell for help but she knows a Wanda sneeze from ten miles away. It is like the call of a baby monster to its mommy. Brenda took one look at Wanda and screamed. Then she scooped her up, saying, "Oh, Wandy-Woo-Woo" (which is the icky name Brenda calls Wanda if she can't find Pusskins to fuss over). "My poor baby. Come and get dry before you *catch your death*." And all the time she was saying that, Brenda was staring at me as though I had tried to drown Wanda instead of save her.

After Wanda had been led away by the mommy monster—and had not even said, "*Thank you, Araminta, for rescuing me*"—Aunt Tabby looked at me in the same way that Brenda had. "I am disappointed in you, Araminta," she said. "I had hoped you were growing out of your bad habits, but it seems you still enjoy these childish practical jokes. They are *not funny*, Araminta. Much as I do not like to admit it, I think your great-aunt Emilene has a point. Boarding school would *do you good*."

With that, Aunt Tabby swiveled on her heel like a clockwork soldier and marched off. I stared at her pointy, cross shoulders as they disappeared through the moldy curtains at the end of the corridor and heard her boots clomping down the stairs. Now I knew what Wanda felt like. I felt as though Aunt Tabby had thrown a bucket of cold water over *me*.

~2~

SCUPPERED SUPPER

It took Wanda ages to escape from Brenda's clutches. I was sitting in our Thursday bedroom listening to a brilliant thunderstorm and reading the bat book *Beastly Bats*, which I had borrowed from the Spookie Library-on-Wheels that stops outside Spookie House every Monday. I love the Library-on-Wheels—they have the best books ever. I was reading about werebats when Wanda, escorted by Brenda, came in with her hair braided and covered in ribbons, just like one of the plastic ponies that she keeps beside her bed.

"Neigh," I snorted.

"Oh, ha-ha, very funny," said Wanda.

"Araminta," said Brenda in a very stern voice. "Wanda's hair is now bat-proof, so perhaps that will put a stop to your bat jokes."

"But I don't *know* any bat jokes," I said. "Well, apart from that one that goes, 'What do you call a ten-foot-tall bat carrying a machine gun?'"

"What *do* you call a ten-foot-tall bat carrying a machine gun?" asked Wanda.

"Sir," I told her.

Wanda looked at me, puzzled. "Why?" she asked.

Brenda heaved a big sigh and Wanda said, "It's all right, Mom, you don't have to stay. I will be okay, I promise." Wanda waited until Brenda had stomped off, then she tugged out her braids and shook her head like a real pony. "I'm sorry, Araminta," she said. "I was only doing a bit of detective work to help you out. I thought I would have a look in the bat turret. So I opened the door, only a tiny little bit, and all the bats just burst out."

"Well, it would have been nice if you had told Brenda that," I said. "And Aunt Tabby."

"I did. Honestly I did," Wanda said. "I told Mom while she was doing my hair, but she didn't believe me. And then I told Aunt Tabby when she came to see if I was all right. And she didn't believe me either."

"Huh," I said. And I carried on reading.

Wanda sat for a while staring at me like she does when she is thinking. I am used to it now, so I didn't take any notice. Suddenly Wanda said, "You look sad, Araminta."

"No I don't," I said.

"Yes, you do. Aunt Tabby has said something horrible to you, hasn't she?"

Now, Uncle Drac once said something about Wanda. He said she was empathetic. I was cross with her at the time, so I agreed. I said I thought she was totally pathetic. But Uncle Drac said that wasn't what he meant. What he had meant was that Wanda always seems to understand how you are feeling. I suppose he was right. So I told Wanda what Aunt Tabby had said about the boarding school. Wanda stared at me and looked puzzled. I sighed. I wasn't getting the sympathy I had hoped for. I decided that Wanda wasn't empy-thingy at all.

Then Wanda said, "Araminta, what is boarding school?"

"It's a school where you go to live," I told her.

Wanda's eyes looked like they were about to pop out. Just like my old goldfish used to when I forgot to top up the tank with water. "You have to live at *school?*"

I nodded. "Yes."

"What—*forever?*"

"Yes. Although I think they sometimes let you out for the holidays if you have been good."

"Oh, Araminta, that's *awful*," Wanda said. "Because you would *never* be good, and so they would *never* let you out."

I reckoned that Wanda was probably right. Which was bad, because then the Mystery of the Forbidden Bat Turret and the Mystery of the

Terrified Bats would never be solved, as Wanda is no use with Mysteries at all.

Wanda's eyes went all fuzzy like they do when she is going to cry. "So I would never see you again," she said. "Well, not until we left school, and then we wouldn't even recognize each other because we would both be so *old*. Oh, *Araminta*," she wailed.

I felt a bit like wailing myself by now, so it was a good thing that we got interrupted by the sound of Aunt Tabby banging the gong far below in the hall to tell us to come down for supper.

Boowoom-boowoom! Boowoom-boowoom!

Wanda squeezed my hand. Wanda's hands are always a little bit sticky; I think it is all the gummy bears she eats. She looked at me very seriously, like I was dangerously ill or something. "You will have to be really polite at supper, Araminta," she said. "I know it will be difficult, but don't worry, I will help you." And then she squeezed my hand again and I had to go and wash it in the drowned-nun-in-the-bath-bathroom.

On the way downstairs we met Sir Horace and Fang. Sir Horace is a lovely ghost; he lives inside a suit of armor and has a very spooky, booming voice. I was pleased to see him because recently he has been spending more time at his old castle down the road. But Sir Horace does not like thunderstorms and he especially does not like lightning, which I suppose has something to do with living inside a metal suit. So when there is a thunderstorm you can always find him at Spookie House.

"**Ah, good evening, Miss Spookie. Good evening, Miss Wizzard,**" he boomed.

Wanda is still a bit shy with ghosts so she just smiled, but I said, "Good evening, Sir Horace," very politely. This was not because I was practicing for being polite at supper but because you must always be polite to ghosts. And anyway, Sir Horace is always polite to me, so it is only fair.

Fang wagged his ghostly tail while Sir Horace, who is almost as polite as I am, began to bow. There was a horrible, teeth-on-edge creaking noise and Wanda looked at me in a panic. The problem with Sir Horace bowing is that his head falls off. And when his head falls off at the top of the stairs, it bounces all the way down. And Aunt Tabby always blames *me*.

"No, Sir Horace!" I said. "Please don't b—" But it was too late.

Boiiing! Sir Horace's head fell off. But Wanda was ready; she dived and caught it just before it hit the top step.

"Oh, well caught, Miss Wizzard," said Sir Horace. He plonked his head back on and gave it a sharp twist. He chuckled. **"A knight in distress saved by a fair damsel. Ho-ho."** I think it was some kind of ghost joke. Wanda giggled like she understood it, but I reckon she was just showing off.

"And what, pray, can I do for you fair damsels in return?" he asked us.

I was just about to ask him to get rid of Great-aunt Emilene for us—I hoped he might be able to throw her out of a window or something—when Wanda suddenly stopped being shy and got in

first. "Can you help Araminta to be polite at supper, please?" she asked.

Sir Horace chuckled again. **"Oh, I had hoped for an easy task, Miss Wizzard, ha-ha. But fear not, I am at your command. Lead on."**

In honor of Great-aunt Emilene's visit, Aunt Tabby had arranged for us to have supper in the ballroom. The ballroom is huge. It is where my guinea pig, Gertrude, lives, although I haven't seen her for ages.

Wanda and I arrived in style—Sir Horace clanked in with Wanda on one arm and me on the other, and Fang trotted in front like a guard of honor. Edmund had turned up too, so he followed us, floating a few feet above the floor. It was very dramatic and everyone looked at us— even Great-aunt Emilene. My great-aunt can't see ghosts at all, but even she could not miss a walking suit of armor.

"Goodness!" she tutted. "No wonder the child is overexcited all the time."

We smiled graciously and took in the scene. It

looked amazing, like something from one of those vampire films that Aunt Tabby likes to watch. (Actually, Wanda and I like to watch them too, from behind Aunt Tabby's sofa, but she doesn't know that, so you mustn't tell her.) The long table that lives beside the wall was in the middle of the room with some old embroidered curtains over it as a cloth. The chairs around it looked like chair ghosts because they had long white sheets over them, and in the middle of the table was a huge candelabra—which is a kind of metal-tree thingy that you put candles in—and all the candles were alight.

I could see the thin, spiky shape of Aunt Tabby at one end of the table and the fatter shape of Great-aunt Emilene at the other. Brenda and Barry were sitting at Aunt Tabby's end, and Uncle Drac was lurking in the shadows, which is something he does really well. I wondered why Aunt Tabby was allowing him to lurk at supper because usually she tells him, "Stop hanging around, Drac, and make yourself useful for

a change," but then I realized that he was doing something useful. He was pulling up the little elevator that is called the dumbwaiter. You use it to bring food up from the kitchen, and whatever was on its way smelled delicious.

So, as Fang, Sir Horace, and Edmund escorted us to the table and everyone (except Great-aunt Emilene) smiled at us, I actually thought that supper was going to be good.

How wrong can you be?

Great-aunt Emilene smells of mothballs, and the double-ended ferret makes me feel sick, so I was not exactly thrilled when Aunt Tabby told me to sit next to her. "*Me?*" I said.

"Yes, Araminta, *you*," Aunt Tabby replied.

I was going to tell Aunt Tabby about the double-ended ferret and how I would not be able to eat any supper if I sat next to Great-aunt Emilene, when I caught sight of Wanda—who was sitting at the other end of the table with Brenda and Barry—making her *please try to be good, Araminta* face. So I sat in the chair next to the double-ended ferret. Uncle Drac came to my rescue by sitting opposite me, and I felt a bit better until I remembered that Uncle Drac still calls Great-aunt Emilene "Mummy," which always makes me laugh, however hard I try not to.

Brenda had cooked supper, and Brenda's cooking is delicious. It was my favorite too: rat in a blanket. This is not a real rat (although that might taste nice). It is a big roll of meatloaf wrapped in cheesy pastry. Brenda had also done some rat gravy along with a big dish of rat-poo peas, which are peas with butter and mint and nothing at all to do with rat poo, but I like calling them that because it annoys Aunt Tabby.

I was busy squashing the rat-poo peas into the gravy when Great-aunt Emilene leaned over and barked in my ear, "Manners!"

It was a real shock. I jumped; my fork went up in the air like a catapult and a shower of rat-poo peas went all over Great-aunt Emilene's dead ferrets.

"Bertie!" she screeched. "Basil!" Which I suppose was what the ferrets were called before they got sewn together. She jumped up from her seat, pulled Bertie and Basil off her neck, and shook the peas out. A shower of dead ferret fur fell onto my rat in a blanket. Yuck!

Wanda's *please try to be good, Araminta* expression was going full blast now. I knew Wanda thought I was going to say something really rude to Great-aunt Emilene about the ferret-fur sprinkles on my rat in a blanket but—as Uncle Drac likes to say, because for some reason he thinks it is funny—Wanda misunderestimated me. I can be very good when I want to be, and right then I really did want to be good. There was no way I wanted to end up at boarding school.

So, in an extremely gracious and polite way, I turned to Great-aunt Emilene. "Oh, Aunt Emilene," I said. "I am so *very* sorry about the rat poo, I—"

"The *what?*" said Great-aunt Emilene, still shaking out her horrible dead ferrets.

"*Rat poo!*" I said much louder, because she was clearly deaf.

Great-aunt Emilene looked shocked. "Araminta Jane, when I was a little girl I would have been sent straight to bed if I had used a word like that."

Now I hate it when someone calls me Araminta Jane. Even Aunt Tabby in her very worst mood has never called me by my middle name. But even so—despite Wanda's amazing *please try to be good, Araminta* face, which was going into overdrive

-34-

now and made me want to laugh—I not only stayed remarkably polite, I also tried to educate my great-aunt. "Great-aunt Emilene, there is nothing wrong with the word 'rat,'" I told her as loud as I could, so she could hear me. "And there is nothing wrong with the word 'poo,' either. Or with the words 'rat' and 'poo' together. Rats do go poo, even though it isn't green like rat-poo peas—well, only if a rat has eaten something really yucky—and actually the poo is not usually round, either, it's more oblong, but I was using what Uncle Drac calls artistic license to—"

"*Aaaargh!* Araminta, stop!" A sudden yell came from the Aunt Tabby end of the table, but it wasn't from Aunt Tabby. It was from Wanda.

"Stop what?" I asked Wanda.

But Wanda did not reply. She just shoved her elbows onto the table (which is not at all polite) and rested her head in her hands like she had a really bad headache. I think she was even moaning a bit, so maybe she did have a headache from sitting next to Aunt Tabby.

I noticed that everyone else had gone very quiet. Even Great-aunt Emilene wasn't saying anything—she was staring at me with her mouth open. This is also very bad table manners because it is not nice seeing people's food inside their mouth, and my great-aunt had a mouthful of half-chewed rat-poo peas.

I decided that the only polite thing to do was to ignore Great-aunt Emilene's lapse of manners and carry on eating the bits of my rat in a blanket that did not have dead ferret fur on. I was so busy fishing out the little bits of fur that I did not see that Sir Horace had decided to come and give me some advice. So when his ghostly voice boomed out of his armor like a foghorn in my ear, saying, **"When in a hole, Miss Spookie, stop digging,"** it is not surprising that I got another shock.

I am not sure exactly what happened next, but I think I must have turned around really fast because my elbow hit Sir Horace and he began to topple. I jumped up from the table because I knew that when Sir Horace falls over he ends up in hundreds of pieces and it takes ages to get him back together.

"Manners!" Great-aunt Emilene screeched again. I thought she was yelling at Sir Horace, because it is definitely *not* polite to creep up on people when they are eating and boom in their ear. Then she did something very rude indeed. She got up, grabbed hold of me, and tried to push me back in my seat.

Well. I was not pleased. There was Sir Horace

lying in pieces on the floor, groaning and needing help, while this horrible woman with her dead ferrets swinging in my face had grabbed hold of the back of my dress. I was stunned. How would she feel if I had done that to her when she was trying to help an old friend who had fallen to bits on the rug?

Everyone else—even Uncle Drac—just stared with their mouths open. It was Fang who tried to come to my rescue. I suppose dead double-ended ferrets are an exciting thing for a dead dog. Anyway, Bertie and Basil were dancing around in the air and Fang leaped up and bit them. Of course, being a ghost dog, his teeth went right through them, but because I am a nice, considerate person, I thought that Great-aunt Emilene would not like even a ghost dog biting her dead ferrets, which she was clearly very fond of. So I pushed Fang out of the way. Fang is a very realistic ghost, and in the excitement of the moment I had forgotten that he was a ghost. So my push landed on Great-aunt Emilene. She staggered back, tripped over Sir Horace's left foot (it is always his left foot that causes trouble), and went sprawling onto the floor.

"*Araminta!*" Aunt Tabby yelled and jumped up from the table—along with everyone else.

After we had picked Great-aunt Emilene up from the middle of Sir Horace and dusted down her ferrets, the rest of supper was very quiet indeed. All you could hear was the scraping of knives and forks on plates. Even Brenda's tasty apple crumble and custard did not make any-one smile. So when at last Aunt Tabby said, "Araminta and Wanda, it's time for bed," I was really pleased.

As soon as Wanda got outside the ballroom she burst into tears. "Oh, Araminta," she said. "Now you're definitely going to boarding school."

"Don't be silly, Wanda," I told her. "Of course I'm not."

But as we climbed all the way back up to our Thursday bedroom, I wasn't as sure as I sounded.

~3~
STAKEOUT

I didn't sleep very well that night. It wasn't because of the boarding school stuff; it was because of a lot of very strange noises going on in the house. There were thumps and bumps, amazingly loud bat-flapping noises, and I am sure I heard some rude words from Aunt Tabby. I tried to wake up my sidekick but she just said, "Go 'way, 'Minta." But when there is a Mystery to solve, a good detective does not ignore an important lead—so it was up to Chief Detective Spookie to investigate on her own.

I got out of bed, tiptoed to the door, and peered down the hall. I heard Aunt Tabby yell, "Here, Drac, here!" and then I saw Uncle Drac rush past holding out the most enormous bat-catching net. Unfortunately he saw me and skidded to a halt. He seemed very flustered.

"Minty!" he said. "What are you doing awake? Go back to bed. Lock the door and don't come out until morning." And he wouldn't go until he heard me bolt the door.

So Chief Detective Spookie went back to bed with another Mystery to think about—the Mystery of the Bat Net in the Night.

※

In the morning, when I woke and peered out to see what was happening, I found Sir Horace sitting outside. I guessed Aunt Tabby must have put him back together, which she is quite good at. I asked Sir Horace what he was doing and he said, **"I am protecting damsels in distress, Miss Spookie."** He wouldn't tell me any more than that, no matter how much I asked. So that was another Mystery—the Mystery of the Barricaded Bedroom. They were coming in fast.

Wanda wouldn't say much that morning either. I could see that she was still thinking about boarding school, but I had more important things to think about—I had Mysteries to solve.

Chief Detective Spookie now had two suspects. Number-One Suspect was Uncle Drac because I had actually seen him acting very suspiciously, and Number-Two Suspect was Aunt Tabby, because I had heard her acting very suspiciously. I was really excited, because I had what detectives call "a lead." This means that you have found something or someone that might lead you to solving the Mystery.

The first thing you have to do with suspects is interview them. I tracked down my Number-One Suspect to the furry bathroom at the end of the little corridor that leads to the fire escape. He was in his flowery sleeping bag, which he had hung up inside the linen closet and then closed the door. It seemed to me that Uncle

Drac did not want to be interviewed, but there is no hiding from Chief Detective Spookie. You may wonder how I managed to find my Number-One Suspect. I don't usually give away detecting secrets, but because some of you who are reading this may one day want to be a detective—in fact, I might even employ you in Spookie's Detective Agency—I will let you in on a detecting secret: if you are looking for someone who is asleep and you hear snoring, follow the snores and you will find them.

Uncle Drac snores *really* loudly, so I easily found him. However, I would not recommend interviewing a suspect while he is hanging up in a sleeping bag inside a linen closet. The suspect will tell you to go away and then disappear down into the sleeping bag. Even when you prod him with the toilet brush he will not tell you any-thing that makes sense. He will just say stuff like, "Eurgh . . . Go away, Minty" and "For goodness' sake, Minty, give it a rest, will you?"

But a good detective is not put off. I left my

Number-One Suspect to think things over, and as I walked back along the little corridor that leads into the main part of the house, I realized that I hadn't seen any bats hanging around. So I deduced that Uncle Drac had managed to catch them all last night and put them back in the bat turret. Deducing is when you use clues to guess something and it is a skill that all detectives need.

However, I also realized I had not actually solved any Mysteries. There was still the Mystery of the Traveling Sleeping Bag, the Mystery of the Terrified Bats, the Mystery of the Forbidden Bat Turret, and now we had the Mystery of the Bat Net in the Night *and* the Mystery of the Barricaded Bedroom.

When I told my sidekick this she said, "There are too many Mysteries, Araminta. Why don't you just make them into one big one?"

"Mysteries are not like gummy bears, Wanda," I said. "You can't just put lots of different ones into one packet."

"Why not?" asked Wanda. "Maybe that is where they all belong."

I sighed. That was *no* help at all. I had a whole stack of Mysteries piling up far too fast for even a trained chief detective to solve, let alone a detective-in-training with a dozy sidekick.

I sat down on a windowsill behind some moldy old curtains and considered what to do. I still had my Number-Two Suspect to interview, but unfortunately this was Aunt Tabby and I knew she would not tell me anything. So I decided to do what we detectives call a *stakeout*. A stakeout is where you keep watch on something suspicious without anyone noticing you. For a stakeout you need three things.

The first is something to stake out. I decided to go back to the original scene of the crime, which was the little red door to Uncle Drac's bat turret.

The second thing you need for a stakeout is somewhere to hide. Lots of detectives have old vans or run-down cafés to sit in, but seeing as there is not a run-down café in Spookie House and I could not get Barry's old van up the stairs (and even if I did, Aunt Tabby would be sure to notice it), I made do with sitting on the pirates' chest behind the moldy curtain, near the little red door. It gave me a good view of the door but was really dark and shadowy, like a place for a stakeout should be.

The third thing you need for a stakeout is a cover. A cover is something that, if people get nosy, gives you a reason for being there. For example, if you were sitting in a café you would have a cup of coffee. My cover was my book called *Beastly Bats*, and my cover story, just in case I needed it, was that I was waiting for Wanda. Because it was so dark I was wearing the present that Uncle Drac had brought me back from vacation. It was a headlamp and on it was written: *A Present from the Caves of the Werebats*.

I enjoyed being on the stakeout. I sat on the pirates' chest with my headlamp switched on,

and under the cover of reading my bat book I watched and waited for something to happen. And soon something did. I heard Aunt Tabby's boots clomping up the stairs. Aha, I thought, here comes Number-Two Suspect. I switched off my headlamp at once.

Unfortunately Number-Two Suspect was *very* nosy. I think she must have seen my feet sticking out or something because she pulled back the curtain and said, "What are you *doing*, Araminta?"

I had my cover story ready. "I am reading my book while I wait for Wanda," I told her.

Aunt Tabby frowned, and I could see she did not believe me. I sighed. It looked like my stakeout was not going to work, so I decided that I might as well interview my Number-Two Suspect. I switched my headlamp back on and looked up so that the light pointed straight at Aunt Tabby. Aunt Tabby's face was weird, lit up from below. She looked like someone out of one of the vampire movies that she likes watching. Not the beautiful heroine—obviously—but one of the ancient victims, who has been living in the cellar for hundreds of years and has just been discovered by the hero. If I hadn't known it was Aunt Tabby, I think I would have screamed just like a beautiful heroine. However—as Uncle Drac says—I am made of stronger stuff, so I did my scary smile just for fun. I do wish that I had little pointed teeth like Uncle Drac. I think it would make my smile much better.

"Turn that thing *off*, Araminta. I can't see," Aunt Tabby said irritably. "Why do you have to wait for Wanda *here*?"

I did not answer because it was what we detectives call a leading question. This means that if you answer it, you give the game away. Anyway, as chief detective it was my job to *ask* the questions, not answer them. It was then that I noticed that Aunt Tabby was carrying some planks, a large hammer, and a bag of nails. I smiled. My stakeout had been successful after all. I had caught Number-Two Suspect acting in a suspicious manner. So I tried a leading question myself.

"What are those planks and nails for, Aunt Tabby?" I asked.

"They are to put a stop to this nonsense," Aunt Tabby said.

Aha, I thought. Aunt Tabby definitely knows something. "What nonsense, Aunt Tabby?" I asked, and then I yawned so as not to appear too interested in the answer. Some suspects will be lulled into a false sense of security if they think you are not listening properly. However, this did not work with Aunt Tabby.

"Nothing for you to worry about, Araminta," she said, and she zoomed off to the little red door. In three seconds flat she was nailing the planks across it.

Bang, bang, bang!

Bother, I thought. My cover was blown—which means Aunt Tabby knew where I was hiding now—and I hadn't found out anything at all.

Bang, bang, bang! The noise from Aunt Tabby's hammering echoed through the house.

Wanda came to see what was happening.

"Hello, Araminta," she said. "Why are you wearing a headlamp?"

Bang, bang, bang!

I did not reply. A chief detective does not discuss a case with her sidekick in front of her Number-Two Suspect.

Bang, bang, bang!

And then Uncle Drac arrived, all rumpled from getting out of his sleeping bag too fast. He looked very upset when he saw what Aunt Tabby was doing.

"Tabby, stop!" he said. "Please. *Don't*. My poor bats won't have a chance in there if that——"

Aunt Tabby swung around. She was holding three nails between her teeth and she looked fierce. She spoke out of the corner of her mouth, like a real villain. "Drac Spookie. I have been up *all* night. I have searched this house from top to bottom and the . . ."—she stopped and pointed at Wanda and me as if to warn Uncle Drac we were there—". . . *you-know-what* is definitely not in the house." She turned around and began hammering again.

Bang, bang, bang!

"And if the *you-know-what* is not in the house," said Aunt Tabby, "then it must be in the bat turret. And if the *you-know-what* is in the bat turret . . ."

Bang, bang!

". . . then that . . ."

Bang!

". . . is where the *you-know-what* is jolly well going to stay!"

Bang, bang, bang, BANG!

"But my bats!" Uncle Drac yelled. "What about my bats?"

Aunt Tabby swung around, clutching her hammer like she was looking for something else to hit. "The bats will have to take their chances, Drac," she hissed. "Just like *we* have all had to ever since you brought that wretched thing back."

Uncle Drac pointed at us now. "Shush, Tabby, we agreed we wouldn't tell them."

Wanda, who is very nosy, piped up. "Wouldn't tell them *what*?"

I sighed. Sometimes I think I may not be employing my sidekick for very much longer. If we had listened for just a little while more, our suspects would have given themselves away and the mystery would have been solved right there and then. But Wanda had stopped all that with her silly question. And I knew exactly what Aunt Tabby was going to answer. So I said it with her.

"That is for me to know and you to wonder," we both said.

Aunt Tabby frowned at me, but Uncle Drac

didn't even notice. He was still desperate about his bats being shut in the turret. "Please, Tabby. My poor bats. You can't do this to them."

"Well, I just *have*," Aunt Tabby replied in the voice she usually uses with me.

Uncle Drac tried another tack. "Look, Tabby," he said in the kind of voice you use when a horse is about to tread on your foot and you are trying to get it not to. "Look, Tabby, the—er— *you-know-what* could still be out here. It's very tiny, you know. And extremely good at hiding in dark places."

"And I am extremely good at *looking* in dark places," said Aunt Tabby. She picked up the hammer and nails. "I am not discussing this any more." She stalked off with her pointy nose in the air and walked straight into Great-aunt Emilene. Aunt Tabby let out a little shriek and dropped the hammer.

I suppose all the banging noises meant that none of us had noticed her arrive, but suddenly my great-aunt and her dead ferrets were standing

there, staring at the bat door covered in planks. It was very creepy.

"The trunk is packed," Great-aunt Emilene said.

I was suddenly very suspicious. "Trunk? What trunk?" I asked. But no one answered me.

My great-aunt Emilene ignored me and carried on. "Tabitha, I have placed everything that will be required in the trunk. However, I have left it open for you to check."

Aunt Tabby glanced at me; she looked a bit

guilty, I thought. "I don't need to check, thank you, Emilene. I'm sure you have thought of everything. Drac, go and lock Araminta's trunk, will you?"

I jumped up. "*Araminta's* trunk? What trunk? Why? Why is it *packed*? Where am I *going*?"

Wanda just stared at me. Her eyes were very round and glistening and her bottom lip looked a bit trembly.

Uncle Drac's expression reminded me of Brenda's cat when it is about to be sick. As he shuffled past me he muttered, "Sorry, Minty. It's for the best."

I watched Uncle Drac walk slowly down the stairs. "Aunt Tabby," I said. "You have to tell me. *Why have I got a trunk?*"

My aunt took a deep breath. "Because, Araminta, you are going to boarding school."

Wanda said it for me. "No!" she yelled. "No! You can't send Araminta to boarding school. You *can't!*"

SETUP

This was what we detectives call a setup. That is when a chief detective has been ganged up on by people who have secretly plotted to make something bad happen to her.

I had been well and truly set up.

I knew this because Aunt Tabby had my school uniform ready and waiting in our Friday bedroom, which meant that she had been planning this for ages. So while Uncle Drac went to find the key for the trunk and Wanda ran downstairs crying like a baby, I had to put on a horrible school uniform. There was a black tunic with a red sash, and a black blazer with a badge on the pocket that had the letters *GAG* underneath an embroidered picture of the head of a monster with its mouth open. The worst thing was the hat. Now, I like hats. My cousin Mathilda (who is surprisingly nice considering Great-aunt Emilene is her grandmother) makes brilliant hats, and she gave me a wonderful one with dead mice on it for my birthday, but this school hat was horrible. It was made of yellow straw and it had a bright red ribbon around it. It was not subtle at all, not like my beautiful dead-mice hat.

We went downstairs to the hall, and Uncle Drac said he could not find the key to the trunk. He winked at me and I guessed that he was hoping Aunt Tabby would change her mind. But I knew she wouldn't, not with my great-aunt glaring at her. Emilene wasn't going to let a little thing like a lost key stop her from sending me away to a horrible boarding school forever. She took a huge padlock out of her pocket and locked the trunk herself, then she put the key in an envelope, wrote on it, and gave it to me. It said: *Property of Miss Araminta Spookie, c/o Miss Gargoyle's Academy for Girls, Gargoyle Hall. Not to be opened until destination.*

So now I knew where I was going: Miss Gargoyle's Academy for Girls. That would explain the weird badge on my blazer, which I now realized was a gargoyle. I know what gargoyles are because I have read a book called *Ghastly Gargoyles*. They are carved monster heads that live on big old buildings. While I was wondering which one Miss Gargoyle would look like, I heard the *clankety-clank* noise of Barry's van outside in the lane and then the *pop-pop-pop* sound it makes just before it stops.

"Time to go now, Araminta," Aunt Tabby said.

I didn't reply. I decided that I was never going to speak to Aunt Tabby again. Never, ever, *ever* again. But I did say good-bye to Sir Horace, who was standing in his favorite place beside the clock in the hall.

"Good-bye, Miss Spookie," he boomed. "We will meet again. If you are ever in need of assistance, send this kerchief as a message and I will be at your side in a moment." And he slowly raised his arm and placed a red silk spotted handkerchief in my hand.

It was such a sweet thing to do, though I almost wished he hadn't because I very nearly burst into tears. But one look at the double-ended ferrets stopped me from doing that.

"Thank you, Sir Horace," I said. "I will not forget you."

"We will not forget you, Miss Spookie," said Sir Horace. **"Even if we do not meet for another five hundred years."**

That made me feel even worse. Five hundred years might not seem very long to Sir Horace, but it felt like forever to me. I hurried out fast. I patted Fang on his ghostly head as I went and he gazed up at me mournfully, like he knew he would never see me again. I said a quick good-bye to Edmund, who waved gloomily, then I looked around for Wanda.

But Wanda wasn't there. And that made me feel sadder than anything.

Barry and Uncle Drac picked up my trunk. "Oof!" said Uncle Drac. "I don't know what you put in there, Tabby, but it weighs a ton."

"Emilene packed the trunk," Aunt Tabby told him. And then she looked at me in a peculiar way, gave me a lopsided kind of smile, and said, "It has nothing to do with me." It was almost as though she was saying she was sorry.

"I have packed a rather large book for Araminta to read," said Great-aunt Emilene. She smiled at me like a wolf—her yellowing teeth sparkling with spit, her clotted lipstick like blood. "I think you will find it useful, Araminta."

Huh, I thought. I bet it is a horrible book telling me how to be good.

"Now, Araminta, put your hat on," Great-aunt Emilene said. And—would you believe it?—she grabbed the awful school hat out of my hands and stuffed it on my head. I felt so annoyed that suddenly I stopped feeling sad and felt really cross instead. If Aunt Tabby was going to gang up on me with my great-aunt and spend her time secretly planning to send me away, then I didn't want to be at home anymore. I was *glad* that I was going to boarding school. So I walked straight out the door, and as I went I didn't even look at Great-aunt Emilene or Aunt Tabby.

Uncle Drac was waiting by Barry's van. "Good-bye, Uncle Drac," I said.

"It's not good-bye yet, Minty," said Uncle

Drac. "I'm coming too. I'm making sure you get there safely."

Recently, Barry had put three new seats in his van so that Wanda and I could travel in the front together. I got in, took my school hat off and put it on the middle seat, then sat on it. Uncle Drac squeezed in beside me. Aunt Tabby and Great-aunt Emilene came out to wave me good-bye, but I ignored them.

I did look around for Wanda, but she still hadn't bothered to come and say good-bye to me—there was nothing for me anymore at Spookie House.

It was a horrible journey. Barry and Uncle Drac argued all the way. Barry took the road that went along the sea, even though Uncle Drac said we shouldn't. Then, after a while (and a lot of rude words from Uncle Drac), Barry turned off onto a little road that went up into some hills. It was very late in the afternoon and the sun was making long shadows across the fields. The road was very bendy and I was beginning to feel sick, because every time Barry said something to Uncle Drac, he pressed the accelerator angrily and the van shot forward, and when Uncle Drac disagreed, Barry put his foot on the brake. So I was actually pleased when I suddenly saw a signpost with a long, pointing finger. It said: *Gargoyle Hall.*

"There!" I yelled. "There it is!"

Barry slammed on the brake, yanked the steering wheel over, and screeched into the lane. We went bumping along for what felt like miles. Every time Barry zoomed around a bend—which he did a lot—Uncle Drac told Barry what a bad driver he was. And Barry told Uncle Drac to shut up.

At last we got to a huge pair of iron gates with a big sign above them saying, *Miss Gargoyle's Academy for Girls.* Except when I looked closer, someone had crossed out *Girls* and written *Gools.* I smiled. Even I knew that you didn't spell *ghoul* like that.

Barry slowed down—probably because Uncle

Drac was screaming, "Slow down, you idiot! Slow down!"—and the gates opened before us. Barry accelerated through them, past a tiny, boarded-up little house, and we went hurtling up the driveway like there was a whole gang of ghouls chasing us.

It was getting dark and misty, and the van's headlights kept flickering on and off. But every time they went on I could see the shape of a huge house with lots of pointy turrets at the end of the driveway. There were tall trees scattered around and the swirling mist made it look like they were moving. In fact, I think they were, because as we got nearer there was a row of trees on either side of the driveway looking like they had all lined up to see who was coming.

Barry was now busy swerving to avoid pot-holes. Uncle Drac had stopped yelling but now he was groaning in my ear and I was afraid he was going to be sick. Much as I love Uncle Drac, I did not want him to be sick in my ear. So I was quite pleased when Barry did his favorite hand-brake turn and we skidded to a halt on the gravel in front of the entrance.

It was very impressive. Gargoyle Hall was just like a house out of Aunt Tabby's vampire films. It had lots of pointy windows—most of which were dark—and it was almost completely covered in ivy. It had four turrets, one on each corner, and against the darkening sky I could see a whole forest of chimneys soaring up. There were what looked like lots of monsters leaning out from under the roof, but I knew that these were the gargoyles.

Barry got out. A set of very wide steps with lots of columns led up to big double doors at the top. The doors swung open, a beam of light shone out, and I saw a small, round figure in black step outside. She was followed by two identical girls—much taller and thinner—each carrying a large lantern. The three of them stood in a line at the top of the steps staring down at us. They looked very weird, like an apple stuck between two chopsticks.

Uncle Drac got out of the van too, but I didn't

move. I heard the back doors open and the sound of my trunk being dragged out. I heard Uncle Drac shout, "Argh! My foot!" I heard footsteps on the gravel, then grunts and groans, and I guessed Uncle Drac and Barry were carrying my trunk up the steps. And I knew that soon it would be my turn to follow it. Suddenly, I saw a revolting squashy thing pressed up against the van window. Something had come to get me. . . .

"Go away!" I yelled.

The squashy thing stepped back and I saw it was Uncle Drac. Uncle Drac's face has a squishy look to it anyway, but when he presses it against a window (because he thinks it is funny), it looks disgusting. He pulled open the door and said, "Come on, Minty. Come and meet Miss Gargoyle."

"No," I told him.

Uncle Drac got back in beside me. For a moment I hoped that he and I were going to drive away into the night and leave Barry at the school in my place. I smiled as I imagined Barry

Wizzard wearing my school uniform. I shouldn't have smiled, because Uncle Drac said, "Oh, Minty, I *knew* you'd like it here. Miss Gargoyle is an old friend of Mummy's—er, I mean your great-aunt Emilene. And she is very nice. It will be much more interesting for you to be here than at home, and—between you and me—it will be safer, too."

"Safer?"

Uncle Drac nodded. "I am not meant to tell you this, Minty, because Aunt Tabby doesn't want to worry you, but there is a problem with the bats."

"I know that, Uncle Drac," I said. "And I think it is really unfair. It is because I rescued Wanda from the bats that I am being sent away. It is *all* because of the stupid bats."

Uncle Drac looked at me. "Well, Minty, you are half right. It is not because you rescued Wanda, but it *is* because of the bats. Or one bat in particular."

I stared at Uncle Drac. "Which bat?"

Uncle Drac blinked. "I mustn't say any more, Minty. I just wanted you to know that this is not your fault." He sighed. "It is *my* fault. And I am very sorry, Minty. I do hope you will forgive me."

I wasn't sure what it was I had to forgive Uncle Drac for, but I said I would, and he smiled and showed his white pointy teeth. "Well, Minty," he said, "it is time to go up those steps and say hello to Miss Gargoyle." He got back out and held the door open for me. The moment had come. I shuffled across the seat and stepped out onto the driveway. Then Uncle Drac gave me a really sweet little suitcase. "It's your emergency school kit," he whispered, taking my hand. We walked up the steps together. At the top, Uncle Drac pushed me forward. "Go on, Minty," he whispered again.

Miss Gargoyle frowned at me like I had already done something wrong. Then she peered at me through her spectacles and I realized she could not see more than a few feet in front of her. "Ah, Araminta Spookie," she said. "I have heard so much about you. Welcome to Gargoyle Hall!"

Miss Gargoyle was just about the same height as me, although she was a lot wider, and round like a beach ball. With her long black dress she looked as if she had just stepped out of a very old photograph. Her black hair was scraped up into a topknot that had a big pin pushed through it with a small jeweled parrot sitting on the end of the pin. She had tiny eyes like little blue beads that stared at me through her very thick spectacles.

The girls with the lanterns on either side of her did not look nice at all. They were about twice as tall as Miss Gargoyle. They wore long black tunics with white shirts underneath, from which their long, thin necks grew up like stalks. They had sharp, beaky noses and big teeth, and they were identical apart from the color of the sashes around their waists: one was blue and one was yellow. They stared down at me like two vultures.

"Araminta Spookie," said Miss Gargoyle. "Follow me."

I grabbed hold of Uncle Drac to make sure he came too. Miss Gargoyle led the way through a really high entrance hall with a wide staircase sweeping up to a gallery above, and tall columns soaring up to the ceiling. It had a black and white checkerboard floor, and the Vulture girls' shoes made sharp, *clickety-clackety* noises on the tiles as they followed us. Miss Gargoyle led the way into her study, which was a cozy little room with a fire burning in the grate. The Vultures followed us and stood by the door, glowering. I sat down by the fire and Uncle Drac went and lurked by the curtains. Miss Gargoyle brought me a big red book; written on the front were the words: *Gargoyle Academy for Girls. School Register*. Miss Gargoyle opened it and there was a whole page full of names that had been crossed out and had *LEFT* written beside them.

"Sign your name there, please, Araminta," Miss Gargoyle said. She gave me a pen, so I very carefully wrote my name underneath all the crossed-out ones:

ARAMINTA SPOOKIE

Miss Gargoyle smiled for the first time. "Welcome to Gargoyle Academy for Girls." She very carefully locked the register in her desk and put the key to the drawer in her pocket. The two Vultures scowled.

"Now, Araminta," said Miss Gargoyle, "I do

like to get to know my new girls, so I will see you here in the morning at ten o'clock for a little chat. But you must be tired now. Violetta and Philomena, our two head girls, will take you up to your room in the junior girls' corridor."

The two Vultures looked down at me like I was something dead on the ground. *Hmm,* they seemed to say. *Supper.*

Suddenly everything was happening too fast. I grabbed hold of Uncle Drac and dragged him away from the curtains. "Miss Gargoyle," I said, "this is my uncle Drac. And I have to say good-bye to him properly, because I may never see him *ever* again."

"Oh dear!" said Miss Gargoyle. She stepped closer to Uncle Drac and peered at him so that her little blue eyes almost disappeared behind her thick glasses. "Is this Dracandor Spookie?" she asked.

Uncle Drac nodded.

"Dracandor," Miss Gargoyle said, "I am very sorry to hear you are so ill. Emilene never mentioned it." She shook her head anxiously. "You don't look too good, I can see that now."

Uncle Drac looked worried. "Don't I?"

I decided to set Miss Gargoyle straight before Uncle Drac got even more flustered. "Uncle Drac isn't ill," I said. "What I meant was that now that I am here, I won't be going home until I am grown up, so I won't be able to see him until I am really, really old—in fact, I shall be so old that he won't even know who I am."

Miss Gargoyle looked surprised. "Goodness," she said. "You're not going home until you are grown up? Well, well, I've never heard that one before. Now, Araminta, it is the weekend and you will have the school to yourself for the next two days—apart from our head girls, of course." She looked up at the two Vultures nervously. "Matron will bring you some cold supper when you are settled in, and I look forward to our little chat tomorrow. Off you go now."

Uncle Drac gave me a little wave and mouthed, "Bye, Minty."

The two Vultures eyeballed me. "Follow us, Spookie," they said.

So I followed them, into the depths of my boarding school. Into the place I was going to live in *forever*.

~5~

STOWAWAY

This is your room, New Girl," said Vulture with the Yellow Sash.

"It's just you and Matron up here now," said Vulture with the Blue Sash.

"Hur-hur!" The Yellow Vulture laughed like she had swallowed a toad.

They spun around on their metal heels and marched out, slamming the door behind them and making the wooden walls of my room wobble like the sets in Aunt Tabby's vampire films.

I sat down on one of the lumpy beds and

looked around. My room was basic but it was okay. It had a washbasin, two narrow beds, two chests of drawers, and a rail with hangers on it set into an alcove. It was at the very top of Gargoyle Hall, which I liked because it reminded me of my bedrooms at Spookie House and it was actually a lot like our Tuesday bedroom. What I didn't like was that I was there on my own. Before Wanda came to live at Spookie House I was on my own all the time, but I didn't mind because that was all I had known. But when Wanda arrived everything became much more fun, and now I really, really missed her. I stared at my trunk, which was sitting in the middle of the floor, while I listened to the *clickety-clackety* of the Vultures' metal-heeled shoes going down the stone steps at the far end of the corridor. Then the sounds died away and I was alone.

Tap. Tap. Tap.

I jumped up like something had bitten me. *What was that?*

Tap. Tippity-tap.

It was coming from my trunk. Aha, I thought, I know what has happened. One of Uncle Drac's bats has gotten stuck in the trunk. I was quite pleased because I thought it would be nice to have a bat in my cabin for company, but suddenly there was a horrible moaning sound like a trapped ghost.

"*Ooow . . . oooh . . . arooo!*"

Bother, I thought. Edmund is in there. Typical. I would have much rather had Fang or Sir Horace, but I supposed there wouldn't have been room for Sir Horace, and Fang never goes anywhere without him. But I reckoned that any ghost—even Edmund—might come in useful at a boarding school, so I got the envelope with the key to the padlock out of my pocket and undid the lock. The top of the trunk burst open with a *crash*!

Something really horrible jumped out of the trunk.

Ha-ha, just joking. *It was Wanda!*

Wanda went hopping around the tiny room

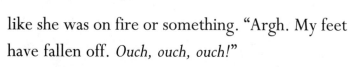

like she was on fire or something. "Argh. My feet have fallen off. *Ouch, ouch, ouch!*"

I could hardly believe that Wanda was actually *there*. I was thrilled to see her but I didn't want to let Wanda know that, because she would have gotten annoyingly big-headed about it. "Be quiet, Wanda, you total dingbat," I told her. "You'll get the Vultures back and then you'll be sorry."

Wanda threw herself down on my bed and started rubbing her feet. "Ooh, I'm on pins and needles," she moaned.

Suddenly we heard the *thud-thud-thud* of heavy footsteps coming along the corridor. Wanda looked at me all googly eyed. "Are those the Vultures?" she asked.

"No, silly. The Vultures have clicky-clacky claws," I told her. "This is someone different. Probably some kind of monster."

"*Monster?*"

"Yes. So you have to hide."

I pushed Wanda underneath my bed, pulled out the top cover, and draped it down so that it hid the space below. I was just in time, because as soon as I had finished, the door flew open and a square-looking person strode in carrying a tray. I wasn't totally sure if the person was a man or a woman. Its face looked a bit like a brick, plus it had very short hair and what Aunt Tabby calls a "five-o'clock shadow"—which is what Uncle Drac gets when he can't be bothered to shave. But the square person was wearing a blue dress with a little white collar, so I guessed it was probably female.

"Arvy Minta," the square person said in a very strange accent. "Velcome to Gargoyle Academy for Girls. 'Ere is your supper." She put a tray down on one of the chests of drawers, then she stepped back and looked at me. She had little green eyes that reminded me of peas fresh out of the pod, and despite the scary haircut she looked surprisingly friendly. "I zink you vill be *verrr* 'appy 'ere," she said. "You look like a Gargoyle kind of girl."

"Oh! Er, thank you . . . ," I said. I was not

sure if it was a compliment to be a Gargoyle kind of girl.

"You may call me Matron," said the square person. "I have a room at ze end of ze corridor. If you are frightened, you vill knock on my door."

"Oh." I wondered why she thought I might get frightened.

Matron glanced over her shoulder as if to check that no one was listening. "Now, Arvy Minta, ze night roars are nothing to worry about," she said. "I can assure you that we do not have *any* monsters in Gargoyle Hall. Not even a leetle one. We have a zero-tolerance monster policy in operation. Sleep vell."

With that, Matron was gone, *thud-thudding* along to the other end of the corridor. I heard the bang of a door closing—it sounded like the door to a bank safe—and then the clank of four heavy bolts being shot home. Zero tolerance of monsters or not, Matron was taking no chances. I was *so* glad that I was not alone right then. Good old Wanda, I thought.

The supper was very nice. We had a flask of hot chocolate, some orange juice, egg sandwiches, some squishy cakes, a bag of grapes, and a huge bar of chocolate. And when I opened Uncle Drac's little emergency suitcase, I found that—apart from a box labeled EMERGENCY KIT—it was full of packets of cheese and onion chips. Perfect.

After we had finished supper, I began to unpack my trunk. A really tiny and very sweet blue bat with cute orange eyes flew out and fluttered around the room. Wanda dived under the bed and would not come out until it had hung itself upside down on the curtains.

"I don't see why you are making such a fuss," I said. "You've been in the trunk with it for hours."

"But I didn't *know* it was in there," Wanda said.

I thought that was probably a good thing, as I wasn't sure Wanda would have been brave enough to get into my trunk with a bat.

Wanda peered inside it, frowning. "I hope it hasn't pooed on my rabbit costume."

"You packed your *rabbit costume?*"

"Of course I did, Araminta," Wanda said, rifling through my spare school uniform and all the other weird stuff that you seem to need for boarding school. "It is my favorite thing in the whole world."

I could not believe Wanda had brought her stupid rabbit costume to school. Brenda and Barry gave it to her for her birthday and she loves it to pieces, even though she looks really, really silly in it. I watched her pull the costume out and hang it up on the rail in the little alcove. Then I watched her fish around a bit more and take out loads of packets of gummy bears. She piled up the packets beside her bed and said, "Okay, Araminta. The rest of the stuff in there is yours."

I finished unpacking the trunk. At the bottom of it was a huge book like a doorstop, which I guessed was the one Great-aunt Emilene had put in. I picked it up expecting it to be something boring about manners, but it wasn't. It was called *The Complete Casebook of Sherlock Holmes*

and it was by someone called Sir Arthur Conan Doyle. When I opened it I saw it was all about a very clever detective and his slightly dim sidekick. I was so surprised—how did Great-aunt Emilene know? "Look at this, Wanda!" I said. "Isn't it great?"

Wanda smiled, but I could tell she was thinking about something else. I was hanging up my spare uniform beside the stupid pink rabbit suit when she suddenly said, "I expect Mom will wonder where I am."

I was surprised. "Doesn't she know?" Wanda never does anything without telling Brenda first.

"No . . ." Wanda sounded a bit miserable.

"Perhaps you had better call and tell her," I said.

"I don't have a phone," said Wanda. "And neither do you, Araminta."

"There's a really old-fashioned one at the end of the corridor that you have to put money in," I told her. "I'll show you how to use it." I looked in the suitcase that Uncle Drac had given me and, just as I had expected, there were some coins for the phone. Good old Uncle Drac.

We tiptoed down the corridor, heading for the light at the far end by the stairs. The telephone was in an alcove along with a huge pile of old phone books. Wanda stared at the phone numbers written all over the wall. "How do we know which number to use?" she asked. "Do we just keep trying all those numbers until we get the right one?"

Sometimes I wonder how Wanda has managed to survive to the age she is. Brenda and Barry don't tell her anything useful at all. "No, Wanda," I said. "We use the right number the first time."

I put the money in the coin slot and Wanda said, "Where are the buttons?"

"You don't need buttons, you use this." I pointed to a silver disc on top of the phone, which had ten holes in it. "This is a dial," I told her.

In each hole was a number from zero to nine. I put my finger in hole number zero, which was the first number, and dragged the dial all the way around to its stopping place. It made a nice clicking sound.

Wanda looked really impressed. "How do you know things like that?"

"Uncle Drac took me on a Phone Practice Expedition when I was younger. We went to all different kinds of telephones and I had to call Aunt Tabby from every single one. It was really fun." I felt a bit sad talking about Uncle Drac, so I decided not to do so anymore and carried on dialing the number for Spookie House. It took ages for the dial to go around to the little stopping-bit at the bottom and then back up again, but at last I heard the weird *ringy-ring, ringy-ring* echoing far away in Spookie House.

Aunt Tabby picked up the phone. "*Yes? What do you want?*" Aunt Tabby doesn't like answering the phone, and she always says that.

"Good evening, Aunt Tabby," I said very politely, because you must always be polite on the phone. "This is your niece Araminta Spookie calling."

Aunt Tabby gave a funny little squeak. "What are you *doing*, Araminta?"

"I am calling Spookie House, Aunt Tabby."

"I know that," said Aunt Tabby. "But *why*?"

"Because Wanda wants to talk to Brenda."

"*Wanda?*"

"Yes. Would you be so kind as to fetch Brenda, please?"

There was a kind of muffled scream and I heard Aunt Tabby yell, "Brenda, Brenda! Araminta has Wanda!"

There was a sound like an elephant charging down the stairs, and then Brenda shrieked so loudly into the phone that I had to hold it miles away from my ear. When she stopped I said, "Excuse me a moment, please, Brenda. I will pass you over to Wanda."

Wanda took the phone like it was a snake or something horrible and held it away from her ear as well. She didn't say much at all, except for "Yes, Mom," and "No, Mom," and "No, Mom, Araminta *didn't* make me do it." At last, after Brenda's voice had come yelling out of the phone for what felt like hours, Wanda took a deep breath and said, "No, Mom. Actually, I am not coming home. I am staying at school with Araminta. It is very nice here and I have had two packets of gummy bears. Good-bye." And then she put down the phone.

Wow.

"Do you *really* like it here?" I asked Wanda as we walked back to our little room.

"Yes," said Wanda, "I do."

And then we heard it for the very first time.

Raaaaaaaargh!

A loud roar drifted up from the floor below. We stopped and stared at each other. I think I must have looked as googly eyed as Wanda did.

"What was *that*?" whispered Wanda.

"A lion?" I suggested. "Or maybe a tiger? Or possibly even a—"

Raaaargh! Raaaaaaargh!

But Wanda was not listening. She raced up the corridor, threw open the door of our room,

and hurtled inside. I was not far behind, but as I scooted in, the sweet little blue bat fluttered out at the same moment that the door slammed shut. Bother.

Raaaargh! Raaaaaaargh! The roar echoed up from somewhere deep in Gargoyle Hall.

Wanda looked at me with big, googly eyes. "What *is* that, Araminta?" she whispered.

"I don't know," I told her. "But whatever it is, I don't think I want to find out."

"Do you think the whatever-it-is will come and get us in the night?" Wanda breathed.

"Crumbs, Wanda, how do I know?" I said. I wished that Wanda wouldn't ask such scary questions.

"We could barricade the door," Wanda said. "Then if the whatever-it-is tries to get in, it wouldn't be able to get in right away, would it? So it might get fed up, and then even if it had a little rest and tried again, it still might not be able to get in and then maybe it would go away and—"

"Stop!" I said. "I get the point."

So we dragged my trunk in front of the door, and then we went to bed. I lay there listening so hard that I felt like my ears were going to fall off, but even though everything was really quiet, I couldn't get to sleep.

After a while, Wanda said in a whisper, "Araminta."

"Yes?" I whispered back.

"Can I come in with you?"

"Yes."

So we scrunched up together in my bumpy little bed and I was so glad Wanda was there. Even though she kept me awake all night with her knobby knees sticking into me.

~6~
BEASTLY IN THE CELLAR

We were woken up by someone banging on the door so hard that the room walls shook. "Wakey-wakey!" a screechy voice yelled. "Rise and shine."

Wanda sat up with her hair sticking out on end. "Shine what?" she mumbled. "Where?"

The door handle rattled and someone gave the door a shove. I was pleased to see that the trunk did not move.

"Open the door!" yelled the voice outside.

I got up and dragged the trunk out of the way. The Blue Vulture fell in.

"What are you doing?" she asked when she had picked herself up off the floor. "New girls are not allowed to lock their doors."

"It wasn't locked," I told her. "It had my trunk across it."

She folded her arms and said, "New girls are not allowed to put their trunks across their doors either." Then she stopped and looked at Wanda. "Hey," she said. "You weren't here last night."

"Yes, she was," I told her, which was quite true.

"No, she wasn't," said the Blue Vulture.

"I was," said Wanda. "You just didn't see me, that's all."

The Blue Vulture looked at Wanda in a puzzled kind of way. "Huh," she snorted. "Are you trying to tell me you were invisible or something?"

"Well, if you didn't see me, then I must have been invisible," said Wanda. I was impressed. Sometimes Wanda manages to sound quite intelligent.

The Blue Vulture went up to Wanda and glared at her. "Don't get clever with me," she said, "or you might regret it. *Something* might come and get you. *Something* that roars. In the night. Know what I mean?"

Wanda looked like she was staring the Blue Vulture down, but I could tell that really she was too scared to even blink. Actually Wanda was too scared to talk, either, but the Blue Vulture didn't know that. She turned on her pointy little metal heel and marched out, slamming the door behind her so hard that I thought the walls might actually fall down.

"Wow," I said. "That was really good. Now we have the advantage."

Wanda swallowed hard and blinked. "The what?" she squeaked.

"I'll explain later," I said. "But first we have a brand-new Mystery to solve."

Wanda frowned. "But we left all those Mysteries at home. We are at boarding school now and we don't do Mysteries here. What we do here is play games and practical jokes and eat midnight feasts."

You can tell that Wanda is not a true

professional. "Wanda," I said, "a chief detective is always on duty, even if her sidekick isn't. We have the Mystery of the Monster in the Night to solve."

Wanda looked unhappy. "Do we have to? That Mystery was really scary, Araminta."

Suddenly a loud bell rang and I heard Matron's door unbolting and the sound of heavy boots marching down the corridor. She banged on our door and yelled, "Downstairs, girls! Breakfast!"

So Wanda borrowed my spare school uniform and we both went downstairs wearing our funny black tunics with the red sashes and the gargoyle badge. Across the entrance hall was a door with a sign on it saying: DINING ROOM. And in front of the door stood the Blue Vulture, looking at her watch.

"You're late," she said. "You've got five minutes to eat your porridge lumps."

Wanda, who likes food—even porridge lumps—pushed open the door and pulled me inside. There were lots of long, narrow tables with benches along either side, but the place was completely empty. All the other girls had gone home for the weekend. The room smelled of boiled cabbage and potatoes with a whiff of burnt porridge. There were two bowls of porridge on the table nearest the door, so we sat down and stared at the porridge lumps. They were cold and there wasn't even any brown sugar to make patterns with. But Wanda looked really excited. "Wow, Araminta, this is amazing. It's just like boarding school porridge should be! I knew it would be, so I brought supplies. . . ." She rootled in her pocket and brought out a packet of cheese and onion chips and a packet of gummy bears. So we both had our favorite breakfast.

We had hardly finished when the Blue Vulture marched in. She had a nasty smile on her face. "Come with me," she said. "You are on cleaning duty."

"Cleaning?" I said. "But we are at school. We are meant to be learning."

"And playing games and having midnight feasts," Wanda chimed in.

"Don't get clever with me," she said. "It's the weekend. So you don't learn, you clean."

"But I am going to see Miss Gargoyle soon," I said. And then I thought that it would not be fair to leave Wanda alone with the Vultures, so I said, "And Wanda is too."

The Blue Vulture laughed as if I had made a joke. "How cozy," she said. "But unfortunately, Miss Gargoyle is, er, indisposed this morning."

"In the what?" asked Wanda.

"Indisposed. Not well, dumbo," the Blue Vulture snapped. "And she will be *indisposed* this afternoon. And *indisposed* this evening, too. Ha-ha."

The Blue Vulture pushed us out of the dining room and marched us across the big entrance hall. As we went behind one of the columns we nearly bumped into the Yellow Vulture. She was standing outside a door with a sign on it saying: HEADMISTRESS, and it looked to me like she was on guard. It was weird, because there was a big, shiny bolt on the outside of the door, which I was sure I had not seen the night before. The Yellow Vulture glared at us, and as we walked past I saw the handle of Miss Gargoyle's study shake like someone was trying to get out. The Blue Vulture quickly pushed us past and shoved us into a dark, narrow corridor. There was a little door at the end and outside was a mop and bucket. The Blue Vulture took a big key out of her pocket and opened the door. The smell of damp spiders wafted out and I knew this was a cellar.

She flicked a switch. A dim yellow lightbulb lit up some rickety wooden stairs and showed lots of thick black cobwebs with some lovely big spiders in them. I like spiders but Wanda is not so keen, even though I have introduced her to some really nice ones. She stared at a huge spider with hairy legs that was dangling down from the middle of the doorway. The spider stared back. Wanda gulped.

"You"—the Blue Vulture pointed at Wanda—"pick up the bucket."

Wanda picked up the bucket very slowly, not taking her eyes off the spider.

"And the mop, stupid."

"You didn't say to pick up the mop," Wanda said, getting picky like she does when she is nervous.

"I told you, don't get clever with me," the Blue Vulture snarled. She leaned down and her beak touched Wanda's little squashy nose. "Did you hear something last night?"

Wanda nodded. She was staring at the tip of the Blue Vulture's nose—she had gone cross-eyed and looked really funny, but I didn't feel like laughing right then.

"They call it the Beast of Gargoyle Hall. And do you want to know where the Beast of Gargoyle Hall lives in the day?" the Blue Vulture snarled.

Wanda shook her head. "No," she whispered.

Blue Vulture stood up straight again. Wanda's eyes swiveled back into the right place and she stared up at the Blue Vulture like a small rabbit looking at a very big snake. Not that I have ever seen a rabbit looking at a snake, but I know if I did, it would look just like Wanda did then.

"Get cleaning," the Blue Vulture snapped. "You're not coming out until every single spider has gone." She shoved us inside, slammed the door, and turned the key in the lock.

"Excuse me," I said to the spider very politely, because you should always be polite to spiders. "Excuse me, we just want to squeeze by." I steered Wanda around the spider and prodded her gently down the wooden stairs.

The cellar was very gloomy, and so full of cobwebs that you could hardly see the old beams in the ceiling at all. It had bare brick walls and a brick floor, and along one wall big cardboard boxes were stacked. Another lightbulb hung from the ceiling and a whole load of spiders stared down. They did not look very pleased to see us, but I expect that was because they had heard what the Blue Vulture had said. Spiders do not like having their homes demolished, which seems perfectly reasonable to me. I would not like having my home demolished either.

"It's all right, spiders," I told them. "There is no way we are going to get rid of your beautiful webs."

"But, Araminta," Wanda whispered, "if we don't get rid of them we won't be allowed out, and we will have to stay here forever and *ever*."

"No we won't," I told her. "We will find a way out."

"But we are locked in a cellar," said Wanda, staring at the dirty brick walls and the stacks of

old boxes. "We are under the ground and there are no windows. How can there be a way out?"

"There is a way out of everything," I told her. "All you have to do is think about it hard enough and make a plan." I didn't actually have a plan right then, even though I was thinking about it quite hard, but I decided not to tell Wanda that.

Wanda didn't say anything. She put her hand in her pocket and took out a crumpled packet. "Do you want a gummy bear? They help you think."

So I took a gummy bear and began to think.

I hadn't been thinking for very long when we heard something scrabbling behind the boxes. *Scritch . . . scratch . . .*

Wanda grabbed hold of me. "What's that?" she whispered.

"It's probably a little rat," I said.

"I don't think it is very little," Wanda said. "Look—the boxes are moving."

Wanda was right; the boxes in the middle of the stack were slowly being pushed forward toward us. "It's the Beastly," she breathed.

"The what?" I asked.

"You know—the thing that the Vulture said. The Beastly of Gargoyle Hall. This is where it lives in the day. And now it is coming to get us. . . ."

Now, you know that I don't always take a lot of notice of what Wanda says, especially when she has her googly-eyed expression, but just then I reckoned she was probably right.

"We will have to get it first," I whispered back. "Here, take the bucket." I shoved the bucket into her hands.

"Why?" asked Wanda, staring down at the bucket.

"As a shield," I said. "I will keep the mop as a spear."

"I'd rather have a spear than a shield," Wanda hissed.

"Well, you can't. I am good with spears. I have practiced a lot."

Wanda got picky again. "When? I've never seen you."

"You don't see *everything* I do, Wanda Wizzard."

But Wanda would not give up. "It's not fair," she said. "You can't do anything against a Beastly with a bucket."

"You can't do much with a mop," I said.

"More than with a bucket!" Wanda can be quite strong when she is in a panic, and suddenly she wrenched the mop from my hands and shoved the bucket into them. There was no time to get it back. With a loud thud, one of the middle boxes crashed to the ground. For a moment there was a box-shaped hole and I could see something black moving behind it. Then the boxes above fell down, there was a horrible squeal, and the hole disappeared.

"Let's get it!" I whispered to Wanda. I held up my bucket as a shield and Wanda pointed the mop. We were ready.

HELP!

A surprisingly small black Beast covered in spiderwebs pushed its way out from the boxes. Wanda leaped forward and shoved it with her mop. The Beast yelled and fell back into the boxes. Wanda was about to thump it on the head when I shouted, "Stop!"

Wanda swung around with the mop. "Why?" she said. "I am just going to finish it off."

"No!" yelled the Beast. "No! Please stop! It's me."

I knew that voice at once. "Mathilda!" Mathilda

is my cousin who I told you about. She is very nearly grown up, and really cool. She wears black and the most brilliant dead-mice hats and always looks amazing. But right then, lying on the floor covered in spiderwebs and boxes, Mathilda was not looking her best.

"Help me up, you two," Mathilda said crossly. "It's the least you can do."

Wanda and I each grabbed hold of one lacy fingerless-gloved hand and pulled Mathilda up. She brushed some of the mess off her long black coat and looked at us with a frown. "Well," she said. "I go to all this trouble to rescue you and this is the thanks I get."

"We thought you were a Beastly," said Wanda.

"Thank you, Wanda," said Mathilda crossly. "That's very nice. *Not*."

I thought Mathilda was not being fair, and so did Wanda. "But the Vultures made us think there *was* one down here," she told her.

Mathilda stopped looking cross and giggled.

"Vultures! That's *very* good. Hee-hee. I know exactly who you mean."

Even though I was really, really pleased to see Mathilda, I did not understand why she was there—or how she had gotten there. And as chief detective I thought it was my job to ask some questions. "It is very nice to see you, Mathilda," I said politely, because something I have learned from Mathilda is if you are polite you often find out a lot more things than if you are not. "But why were you hanging around behind a pile of boxes in a cellar in a horrible school? It's not something I would want to do in my spare time."

"Duh," Mathilda scoffed, like I had said something really stupid. "I wasn't *hanging around*. I came to see Miss Gargoyle with a message from Grannie—I mean your great-aunt Emilene—and I heard Vile and Foul cackling about locking you in the cellar. So I came to get you out."

"Who are Vile and Foul?" Wanda asked. But I had already guessed.

"Your two Vultures," said Mathilda, with a

giggle. "Violetta and Philomena. Come on, let's get out of here before they hear us."

The boxes had been stacked in front of a little window, which was high up and had shutters across it. That was where Mathilda had gotten in. We very quietly put the boxes back how they were, so that when the Vultures came down to let us out (if they ever did) they would think we had disappeared like a pair of ghosts and get really "weirded out," as Mathilda put it. Then we squeezed behind the boxes,

wriggled out through the little window, and closed the shutters.

We found ourselves in a ditch full of weeds. In front of us was an overgrown garden with tall grass sloping down to a big hedge. Mathilda told us to follow her, so we did. We climbed out of the ditch and crawled through the grass. It was fun; it felt like we were tigers stalking our prey. I was really good at it because when I was little I used to practice stalking Aunt Tabby in the garden at Spookie House. It annoyed her, but I did it anyway because I knew it would be useful one day—and now it was.

We would have easily gotten away without anyone noticing if Wanda hadn't crawled into a patch of stinging nettles. Suddenly there was a loud screech and Wanda leaped up like one of those annoying toys on springs that jump out of boxes and manage to be boring (because you know exactly what they are going to do) but scary (because you don't know when they are going to do it) at the same time.

"Aarrgh!" Wanda yelled.

I should have expected that Wanda would find the only stinging nettle patch in the entire garden, but I didn't expect it, so it was a big surprise. So I jumped up too and yelled, "What? What is it?"

"*Shush!* Get down, you two!" Mathilda hissed.

I got down but Wanda didn't. She was hopping about, clutching her knee. "*Ouch-ouch-ouch-ooh-ooh-ooh!*"

Mathilda grabbed hold of Wanda and pulled her down into the long grass, away from the stinging nettles. Then she very slowly looked up to see if we had been spotted. "Bother!" she whispered.

"Have they seen us?" I asked.

Mathilda threw herself back into the little space of flattened grass that we had made. "The Vultures haven't seen us," she said, "but Miss Gargoyle has. She's waving at us through the window. Bother."

I remembered the rattling door handle of Miss Gargoyle's study and the Yellow Vulture standing on guard outside. "That's because Miss Gargoyle is being held prisoner," I said. "This morning, the Vultures put a bolt on the outside of her study door. She is probably asking for help."

Mathilda looked shocked. "I didn't know it had gotten *that* bad," she said.

Slowly, like a tiger checking out her prey, I raised my head above the grass. I saw the line of tall, pointy windows that ran along the bottom of the house. It was easy to guess which one was Miss Gargoyle's study—it was the window with a small, round person holding up a big sign that read: HELP!

We crawled quickly down the hill and soon we reached the big hedge and a very tall gate, which was locked. Mathilda wriggled through a small hole at the foot of the hedge and we followed her. We came out into a little lane, where a black motorbike was parked. It had an amazing sidecar that looked like a big silver bullet.

As we looked back at Gargoyle Hall, all we could see was the roof with its gargoyles and turrets. It looked really mysterious. "We're safe," Mathilda said. "They can't see us down here. Come on, let's get going."

"Going where?" asked Wanda.

"I'm taking you home," Mathilda said, pointing at the really cool motorbike. "And then I will get some help for Miss Gargoyle."

Yesterday evening I would have been thrilled if Mathilda had turned up on her fantastic motorbike to take me home—but today was different. A good detective does not leave an unsolved mystery behind. And, apart from the Spookie House Mysteries, I now had two Gargoyle Hall Mysteries: the Mystery of the Monster in the Night (which I now knew was really the Mystery of the Beastly of Gargoyle Hall) and a new Mystery: the Mystery of the Headmistress Imprisoned in Her Study. So I said, "No thank you, Mathilda. We don't want to go home."

"Don't we?" asked Wanda.

"No, Wanda, we don't. We want to know what's going on at Gargoyle Hall."

"A load of trouble," Mathilda said. "That's what's going on. I told Grannie that she was crazy sending you here. Come on, get in." She pointed at the sidecar. "I'll tell you all about it when I get you safely home."

Wanda did not need telling twice. She scrambled into the sidecar and sat in the front seat looking really pleased. I wanted to get in but I didn't. I knew that as soon as we got home Aunt Tabby would take over and Chief Detective Spookie would be off the case. This is what happens with detectives. They get started on their investigations and then some bossy lieutenant takes over. I was not going to let this happen to me, especially as Mathilda was my Number-One Witness and I needed to get her to tell me all she knew. Right now. So I said, "Mathilda, thank you very much for your kind offer, but we are definitely not going home. No way."

But my less-than-faithful sidekick said, "Oh, but I *love* this little car thingy. Look, Araminta, it's got such cute red seats. And the blue carpet is gorgeous. Oh, wow, it is even on the inside of the door!"

Mathilda climbed onto the big springy saddle of the motorbike and put on a really cool black helmet with goggles on the top of it. "We're going, Araminta," she said. "Are you coming?"

I needed to stall for time. This is what detectives do when they are in a tricky situation and need to think. So I said, "Okay. But before we go, will you tell Wanda what's going on? Because as soon as we get home Brenda will scoop Wanda up and disappear with her and she will never, ever know."

I could see that Wanda realized I was right. And because Wanda is very nosy and likes to know everything, I could also see she was not as keen on going home right away as she had been. My plan was beginning to work.

"All right," Mathilda said reluctantly. "But you had better get in the sidecar. I want to be able to make a quick getaway if those Vultures appear."

But Chief Detective Spookie was not to be tempted. Even though I really wanted to sit in the shiny silver bullet sidecar, I suspected that once I was in there Mathilda would just zoom off home. So I said, "Thank you, Mathilda, but I will keep watch from here."

Mathilda gave me a strange look. "I wasn't planning on kidnapping you, Araminta."

"Good," I said, but I didn't get in all the same.

I was about to start interviewing my Number-One Witness when my sidekick piped up with, "So who are the horrible Vultures? What makes that scary roaring in the night? Why is Miss Gargoyle locked in her study? How did you *know* we were in the cellar?"

I was quite impressed that Wanda had figured out exactly the questions I was going to ask, but I was not pleased. It is a chief detective's job to ask the questions, not the sidekick's.

Wanda got out another bag of gummy bears and passed them around.

"No thank you, Wanda," Mathilda said. "But

give some to Araminta; then she won't keep asking me questions."

Huh! That was not fair. Mathilda obviously
had not noticed that so far it was Wanda who
had been asking all the questions. But I did not
say anything, because Mathilda had begun to
speak. And a good detective always listens to her
Number-One Witness very carefully indeed.

~8~
NUMBER-ONE WITNESS

L ast year," Mathilda began, "I was head girl at Gargoyle Hall."

"You!" I was amazed. I thought that Mathilda was far too old to go to school. And with her dead-mice hats and motorbike, she didn't seem like the kind of person who gets to be head girl.

"Yes, *me*," Mathilda said, sounding a bit annoyed. "Wanda, give Araminta some more gummy bears, please. I was head girl, and at the beginning of last term the school had a hundred girls in it. By the end of term nearly all of them had left."

"Was that because you were head girl?" Wanda asked.

"No, it was *not*," Mathilda said, sounding even more annoyed. "Why don't you have some more gummy bears too, Wanda?" Mathilda dropped her voice and looked around as if she was afraid of someone hearing. "It was because of the *Beast of Gargoyle Hall*."

"Ooh . . . ," breathed Wanda, digging into the gummy bear packet. "The Beastly! We heard that last night."

"You did?" Mathilda looked shocked.

Chief Detective Spookie decided to ask a leading question before she had some more gummy bears. "Mathilda, what *is* the Beast of Gargoyle Hall?"

"Well . . . there is an old story that Gargoyle Hall was once haunted by a great black beast. But there had never been any sign of it until last term, when we began to hear the most horrible roars in the middle of the night. So I got a group of older girls together to track it down. It wasn't easy to find."

"*Gersts rrrnt*," I said sympathetically.

"What?" said Mathilda.

I managed to prize my teeth apart from the gummy bears. "Ghosts aren't easy to find," I said. "I spent ages exploring Spookie House before I found one."

"So I heard," said Mathilda. "Anyway, we spent quite a few nights searching and eventually we saw it in the distance, lurking at the end of a corridor. It was a huge black thing with lots of arms and a horrible big head. It scared the girls so much that many of them decided to leave." Mathilda sighed. "So that didn't turn out to be a very good idea."

"Did the Vultures hunt the Beastly too?" Wanda asked.

For once I was pleased my sidekick was asking questions, because I had just discovered that if you eat a load of red gummy bears together, they are extra sticky.

"No, they didn't," said Mathilda. Which was what I expected her to say.

"So when did the Vultures arrive?" asked my surprisingly useful sidekick.

Mathilda sighed again. "At the beginning of last term. I remember it well. Because I was head girl, I had breakfast with Miss Gargoyle in her study every Monday morning. Miss Gargoyle was so nice; she always wanted to know what was going on and how all the girls were doing. It was a really happy school and I used to tell Grannie that you and Wanda should go there. Grannie did try to get Aunt Tabby to send you, but she wouldn't. She said she liked having you and Wanda at Spookie House."

I was amazed. Aunt Tabby never gave the slightest sign of liking me being at Spookie House. Ever. But I couldn't say anything because of the red gummy bears.

"Anyway," said Mathilda, "we were just having our buttered toast when Matron bustled in and said that the two new girls had arrived. It was the Vultures. They came in to sign the school regis-ter and they stared at me and Miss Gargoyle like they hated us. I showed them to their room and when I came downstairs, Miss Gargoyle told me all about them. Their father—she called him the Bonkers Baron—owned Gargoyle Hall.

"He wanted to turn it into a luxury leisure center. So although Miss Gargoyle was pleased that he had sent his daughters, because she thought it meant he had given up trying to close the school, she felt kind of worried, too. 'Mathilda, dear,' she said, 'something just doesn't make sense.'

"After the Vultures arrived, the whole atmosphere of the school changed. They stirred up trouble between the older girls and they were horrible to the little ones. So what with the Vultures in the day and the Beast of Gargoyle Hall at night, girls began to leave. One weekend twenty parents arrived to take their daughters away and a whole load of teachers left too. It was awful; Miss Gargoyle was in floods of tears. Later I caught the Vultures laughing in the tuck shop."

"What's a tuck shop?" asked Wanda.

"It's the school shop that sells gummy bears," said Mathilda.

"Wow." Wanda looked impressed.

"Anyway," said Mathilda, "by the end of last term we were down to just me, a few girls, and the Vultures. I had to leave because I was too old, so this term the school staggered on with just a few girls and the horrible Vultures—until yesterday morning, when the last two girls left. Miss Gargoyle was in a terrible panic. She knew that if she didn't find anyone else, then the next day the Bonkers Baron would get his horrible hands on Gargoyle Hall."

"That is awful," I said.

"Yes it is," agreed Mathilda. "Which is why Grannie, who is Miss Gargoyle's best friend, was desperate for you to come to the school. And she knew you would actually *like* the roars in the night and not be scared."

"Oh. I thought it was because Araminta was being bad," said Wanda, sounding a bit disappointed.

"Well, Grannie had to make it seem that way because she was afraid Aunt Tabby wouldn't let Araminta go."

"Uncle Drac has a good word for what people are when they behave like that," I said. "But I can't remember what it is. It begins with a *D*."

"Desperate?" said Mathilda.

"No," I said. "Devious."

Mathilda frowned. She didn't seem to like that word. "Let's get going," she said. "There's no point hanging around here."

But I had a question to ask my Number-One Witness. "Mathilda," I said, "did anyone hear the Beast of Gargoyle Hall before the Vultures arrived?"

"No."

"Thank you. No further questions."

Mathilda gave me a half smile that reminded me of Aunt Tabby. "Well, that's a relief," she said. "Get in, Araminta, and let's get out of here."

One of the things you have to do when you are chief detective is to think fast, which is what I was doing right then. Another thing you have to do is have a really good plan, and suddenly I knew I had one. I took out the red hankie that Sir Horace had given me and passed it to Mathilda.

She looked puzzled. "What's that for?"

"It's for Sir Horace," I said. "It's a message to him that I need help. I think it would be a really good idea if you go back to Spookie House and ask Sir Horace to let us have Fang. Fang will scare the Vultures away. Then we can free Miss Gargoyle and get all the nice girls back to the school."

"You have forgotten about the Beast of Gargoyle Hall," Mathilda said.

"No, I haven't."

"You think the Vultures brought the Beastly with them, don't you, Araminta?" my sidekick piped up. "You think it's their pet and when they go, the Beastly will go too."

"No, Wanda," I said. "I do not think that at all."

What I did not tell Wanda was that actually, I had a hunch that the Vultures were definitely involved with the Beast, but I wasn't going to tell her about it yet. I needed to do a bit more thinking first. All good detectives have a hunch now and then. This is not like a camel with a bump or anything like that. It is a feeling that you know the solution to a Mystery, even if you do not have any proof. And because of my hunch, the Vultures were my Prime Suspects in the Mystery of the Beast of Gargoyle Hall—and Prime Suspects are the most suspicious suspects of all.

"Well, that's what *I* think," said my know-it-all

sidekick. "I think a Beastly is just the kind of pet those horrible Vultures would have."

"We shall have to find out, won't we?" I said. "And Fang is just the ghost to do it. He is a hunting dog, and he will hunt out the Beast of Gargoyle Hall in no time at all."

I could see that Mathilda was thinking hard. "Actually, that is not a bad idea," she said. "All right, then, I'll go and fetch him now. You two lie low until I get back with Fang."

"I'm not lying low in that grass," said Wanda. "It stings."

"I'll drop you off at the porter's lodge by the gate," Mathilda said. "The porter left last term too, after the Beast broke his windows one night. You'll be safe there and out of the way of the Vultures. I'll pick you up when I get back."

"We'll make our own way there, thanks, Mathilda," I said. "We have things to do here first. Come on, Wanda. Hurry up and get out."

Wanda got out of the sidecar very, very slowly, like I was making her do something she didn't want to do. "What things do we have to do?" she asked suspiciously.

I did not answer. A chief detective does not have to tell her sidekick everything.

Mathilda fished around in her pocket and brought out a bag of pink shrimp. "Here, have these while you're waiting," she said. "I'll be awhile."

I love pink shrimp. "Thank you," I said.

Mathilda pulled her goggles down so that she looked like a weird insect. "Keep out of the way of the Vultures, okay?" she said. Then she shoved her foot down on the kick start of the motorbike and it roared even louder than the Beast of Gargoyle Hall. Wanda put her fingers in her ears and we watched Mathilda's amazing motorbike zoom off down the lane in a cloud of dust.

I felt sad to see it go. But when a chief detective is on an important case, she cannot go racing around the countryside in a motorbike side-car, however much she might want to. "Come on, Wanda," I said. "We have a headmistress to rescue."

We crept back up the garden, then we tiptoed along the path at the back of the school, ducking down below the windows. When we got to Miss Gargoyle's window, I very slowly stood up until I could see into the study. The HELP! sign was lying on the floor and Miss Gargoyle was sitting at her desk with her head in her hands. She didn't see me and I ducked back down.

"What did you see, Araminta?" hissed Miss Nosy Bucket.

"Shush," I whispered. "Come on, let's go."

We came to a side door. I tried the handle and it opened. A moment later we were in a gloomy, narrow corridor painted the kind of brown that Aunt Tabby likes and smelling of the kind of cabbage that Aunt Tabby cooks. It felt just like home.

"Araminta, what are we *doing*?" Wanda whispered.

"Like I said, Wanda. We are going to rescue Miss Gargoyle."

"But the Vultures are guarding her."

"So you will have to lure them away."

"*Me?*" Wanda gasped.

"Yes. Then I will undo the bolt and let Miss Gargoyle out."

"But that's not *fair*," Wanda said in the moany voice that Brenda is always telling her off about. "*I* want to undo the bolt and let Miss Gargoyle out."

"Well, you can't. Because you won't be there."

"Where will I be?" Wanda asked suspiciously.

I did not want to tell Wanda that she would be running away from the Vultures, dressed as a pink rabbit. I thought it best to break that to her gently.

PINK RABBIT

No, Araminta. No, no, no!"

We were in our little room in the attic and I was holding up the pink rabbit costume. "Shush," I hissed. "They'll hear you!"

"I don't care," Wanda whispered—so I knew she *did* care, otherwise she would not have whispered. "I am not—repeat, *not*—putting on my pink rabbit costume and calling the Vultures rude names so that they chase me. No *way*."

"You don't have to do rude names if you don't want to," I said. "You can just jump up and down in front of them and waggle your ears or something and *then* run away. They are bound to chase you."

"But I don't want them to chase me."

I sighed. "But that is the whole point of the plan. The Vultures have to chase you so that I can let Miss Gargoyle out."

"Why can't *you* wear the rabbit costume and I will let Miss Gargoyle out?" Wanda asked.

"Because you said that you would never, ever, *ever* in a million years let me wear your rabbit costume," I said. "And I would not want you to break your word."

"But——"

"Besides, you're too short to reach the bolt."

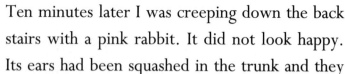

Ten minutes later I was creeping down the back stairs with a pink rabbit. It did not look happy. Its ears had been squashed in the trunk and they now hung down limply. At the foot of the stairs we tiptoed along the gloomy back corridor and stopped outside the cellar door. The key was still sticking out of the lock. I very quietly unlocked the door, took out the key, and gave it to the pink rabbit. "Remember," I whispered, "all you have to do is hop along to Miss Gargoyle's door, jump up and down a bit, and when the Vultures start chasing you, you run into the cellar and lock the door. Then you can get out the way we did with Mathilda. Okay?"

"No, it is *not* okay, Araminta," the pink rabbit said.

"But you *are* going to do it?" I asked.

"I *suppose*," grumbled the pink rabbit.

I led the way along the little creepy corridor, making sure that the pink rabbit was following me. When we got to the end I peered around the corner to the big entrance hall with the four pillars. Brilliant! Both Vultures were outside Miss Gargoyle's door. We tiptoed over and hid behind the nearest pillar.

"Hur-hur," the Yellow Vulture was saying. "Those two little weeds who arrived yesterday won't last another night."

"Not after their day down in the cellar," sniggered the Blue Vulture. "With all those spiders. Hey, Foul, did you see how scared they were?"

"Yeah. That was fun."

"You know, I'll miss this place. Best fun we've ever had. But the job is done."

"So when's Dad coming, Vile?"

"I told him tonight at midnight. I'm waiting until this afternoon when old Gargoyle is desperate for her tea, then we'll do a raid and grab the register."

"But the weed is still signed in, Vile," said the Yellow Vulture.

"Don't worry, Foul. I'll fix that somehow. She won't be on that register by midnight, you can be sure of that. Hur-hur!"

"Ooh, Vile, you are clever."

"Yeah, I am. So it's bye-bye, Gargoyle Academy for stupid girls and silly little weeds!"

The pink rabbit and I looked at each other. The rabbit was as cross as I was. "Weeds!" it mouthed. "We'll show them weeds, Araminta!" It straightened the bent wire in its ears so they stood up properly, and gave me a double thumbs-up sign. I grinned and did the same. Spookie's Detective Agency was in business.

The pink rabbit shot out from behind the pillar and I watched its fluffy white tail bob up and down as it bunny-hopped across the checkered floor. The Vultures stared at it like they had seen a ghost. Their mouths dropped open and stayed that way, and their Vulture eyes went all round and googly, just like Wanda's do sometimes. The pink rabbit was very brave. It hopped right up to them and got so close that I was afraid one of them might grab it—but the Vultures were too surprised to move.

The rabbit waved its arms and yelled out, "Hey, smelly Vultures sitting on a tree, you're so stupid you can't catch me! Hee, hee, hee!" Then it turned and ran. It shot right past me, and I saw it had a big smile on its face. I was afraid for a moment that it would give me away by saying something to me as it ran past, but it didn't even give me a glance. It was a True Professional.

Then the Blue Vulture yelled out, "Grab it!" and they were off. They hurtled by and disappeared into the creepy corridor after the pink rabbit. I really wanted to watch and make sure the rabbit got into the cellar all right, but there was no time to lose. I raced over to Miss Gargoyle's study, undid the bolt, and ran in. Miss Gargoyle hadn't moved since I saw her through the window. She looked up and opened her mouth to say something, but I didn't give her a chance.

"I have come to rescue you," I said. "Come with me. Quick, before the Vultures come back."

Miss Gargoyle understood at once. She jumped to her feet, snatched up the school register from her desk, and, clutching it to her like a baby, she followed me out. As I was bolting the door I heard the *clickety-clackety* of their footsteps coming back. Miss Gargoyle looked at me in panic— there was no time to get out the front doors. She

grabbed hold of me, pulled me across to a closet labeled TRUNKS, dragged me inside with her, and closed the door.

I could not believe a headmistress could be so stupid—she had gotten us both trapped in an even tinier place than her study. Added to that, it was totally dark in the closet; there were no windows. Even though she was the headmistress, I wanted to tell her what a total twit she was, but I couldn't even do that because outside, only a few feet away, were the two Vultures.

"What on earth was that stupid rabbit thing?" one of them was saying.

"Don't be daft, Foul. Didn't you recognize those googly eyes? It was one of the weeds."

"But they're locked in the cellar."

"Not anymore, dumbo. Obviously, they've gotten out."

"Yeah, *right*. They get out and what's the first thing one of them does—changes into a rabbit costume and starts dancing right in front of us? No, Vile, I don't think so."

"Well, I'm going to go and check the cellar. Something's up, Foul. And I don't like it."

I heard Miss Gargoyle *tut-tut* under her breath. Then she reached across me and pressed something in the wall. The floor gave a little lurch and suddenly we were moving. "It's all right, Araminta dear," she said. "It's an elevator. For the school trunks."

Aha, I thought. I knew what Uncle Drac would say just then: Miss Gargoyle is not as green as she is cabbage-looking. Which is a funny way of saying that someone is not as daft as you thought they were.

We got out of the trunk elevator and stepped into our attic corridor. As soon as I closed the elevator door it went back down again—someone had called it.

Miss Gargoyle hurried along the attic corridor with the school register tucked firmly under her arm. "Come along, Araminta," she said. "We are going to see Matron. I need to keep the school register safely under lock and key. I am not letting those—what did you call them, Vultures, was it? Very good, I like that—Vultures get hold of it. Never, never, *never*!"

Now, a good detective always makes sure she has all the facts. And there was one fact I was missing: Why was the school register so important? So I said, "Why do the Vultures want to get the school register, Miss Gargoyle?"

Miss Gargoyle looked at me with her little blue eyes, which were sad beneath her spectacles. "There is what they call a covenant on the use of Gargoyle Hall. It says as long as there is

at least one girl signed in the school register, Gargoyle Hall must be used as a school. This register"—Miss Gargoyle held the fat, red leather book up for me to see—"is an important legal document, and I fear that Violetta and Philomena are not to be trusted. I am not letting this out of my sight."

"Why don't you just expel them?" I asked as we reached Matron's bank-vault door.

Miss Gargoyle looked wistful. I could tell she wanted to. "It's complicated, dear," she said. "I don't want to upset their father. He owns the school, you see. And of course, if I did expel them, you would be the only girl in the school."

"Not the only one, Miss Gargoyle," I said. "My friend Wanda Wizzard is here too. She stowed away in my trunk. And she dressed up as a pink rabbit to be a diversion so that I could rescue you. She would love to be in the school register. In fact, you could put her in right now!"

Miss Gargoyle looked at me and smiled. "Well, Araminta, you do tell me the strangest things.

But I am sorry to say I can't put your friend in the register. She must sign it for herself."

"I could sign it for her," I offered. "I can do her signature really well."

Miss Gargoyle sighed. "That is very kind of you, Araminta, but at Gargoyle Hall we do the right thing and abide by the rules. And to tell you the truth, neither you nor your friend may want to stay for much longer. There is a rumor about a Beast of Gargoyle Hall. It roars at night, and I have to admit I have heard it. And of course, when Gargoyle girls hear it, they don't want to stay at the school anymore."

"We have heard it too," I told her. "We thought it was very interesting. It is nice to have something like that in a school, I think."

"How quaint. But sadly no one else sees it like that."

"I know. Which is why we are going to help to get rid of it for you. And then all the girls who left because it scared them will come back and this will be a school forever and *ever*."

"Ah, the optimism of youth," Miss Gargoyle sighed. "Now, let's see if Matron is in." She knocked loudly on the door.

"Who is it?" We heard Matron's voice trill nervously.

"Open the door, Brunhilde!" Miss Gargoyle shouted. "It is I, Ermintrude!"

There was the clanking sound of all the bolts being drawn and chains being taken off, then Matron opened the door and peered out.

"We are seeking sanctuary," said Miss Gargoyle.

Matron looked blank. "Seeking who?"

"Just let us in, will you?" Miss Gargoyle sounded quite snappy. She glanced over her shoulder anxiously. We could hear the trunk elevator coming back up—a Vulture was on her way. "Step aside, Brunhilde!" Miss Gargoyle pushed me into Matron's room, then she hurried in after me and very quietly closed the bank-vault door.

Matron's room had a sweet little arched window and a squashy sofa, but there was no way I could stay. "Sorry, I've got to go," I said. And before Matron could start turning keys and shooting home bolts, I zoomed out.

I had a pink rabbit to find.

Outside Matron's room I stopped and listened. I heard the trunk elevator arrive and I knew I had to hide—I had a dangerous Prime Suspect looking for me. One of the things you have to do when you are a chief detective is to think fast. And what I was thinking, very fast indeed, was that the first place a Vulture would look was in our room. So, as the door to the trunk elevator banged open, I slipped into the room opposite. Success! The Blue Vulture went *clickety-clacketying* into our room and while she was looking under the beds I crept out and ran to the trunk elevator.

Unfortunately, Vultures have really good hearing. The Blue Vulture poked her beak out of our door. "Oy, weed!" she yelled, and raced after me. But she was not fast enough—I was already in the elevator. I slammed the door closed and frantically pressed the button with *B* for basement on it. And then, to the sound of lots of door rattling and some very rude words, the trunk elevator began to move. And there was Chief Detective Spookie, squished into a dark little box, heading down through Gargoyle Hall, escaping one dangerous Prime Suspect. But was she heading straight for another one?

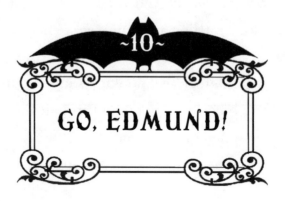

~10~

GO, EDMUND!

The *B* lit up and the elevator came to a stop. Very carefully, I pushed open the door, but it made a really loud creak. Bother. Outside the elevator it was very gloomy and had that damp spider smell, so I knew I was in the basement, which was good. But suddenly, I heard the *clickety-clackety* sounds of Vulture feet coming my way.

"Hey, Vile," a Vulture voice called out. "Did you find old Gargoyle and the register?"

I shot out of the elevator, leaving its door open so that the Blue Vulture couldn't call it back up, then I zoomed around the corner into the shadows.

"Vile? Vile, is that you?" The Yellow Vulture's voice echoed eerily in the gloom of the narrow basement passage.

I tiptoed away—very fast—and saw some steps heading up to a glass-paneled door. Hooray! Through the glass I could see a tree; I was nearly outside. I raced up the steps, pushed open the door, and almost fell out into a grassy ditch. I hurried along the ditch, heading toward where I thought the little cellar window was. I got there just in time to see a pair of pink ears wobbling around, as if they were trying to make up their minds what to do. So I made up their minds for them—I grabbed them and pulled.

"Argh! *Getoffme!*" the rabbit yelled.

"*Shut up, Wanda, it's me!*" I hissed. I gave another massive pull and a very grubby pink rabbit fell into the ditch. "*We gotta get outta here!*" I whispered (because that is what detectives always say). The rabbit nodded, its ears bouncing up and down in a way I would have laughed at if we hadn't had more important things to do right then—like make ourselves scarce. Which is what detectives have to do sometimes when a pair of dangerous suspects has decided to chase them.

"Hey, Foul! I can see them!" came a yell from the Blue Vulture.

"Oh, ha-ha! Look at those stupid ears!" the Yellow Vulture laughed.

The pink rabbit looked really cross at being laughed at, but I grabbed hold of its paw and we headed for the woods bordering the driveway at top speed. Just before the woods there was a fence, but there were lots of holes in it, so I squeezed through and pulled the rabbit after me. Then we raced across to a really big tree and stopped to catch our breath, listening hard for the sound of any approaching Vultures.

"They're laughing," the pink rabbit said.

"Don't be silly; why would they be laughing? Anyway, how come you can hear it and I can't?"

"Because I have big ears."

"Oh, ha-ha. Very funny." I listened a bit harder and I realized that the pink rabbit was probably right. There were some very odd cackling noises coming from the other side of the fence. I peered around the tree to see if the Vultures were following us, but there was no sign of them at all.

Now we had to get to what we detectives call the rendezvous. This is a place where you have agreed to meet someone—and our rendezvous was the boarded-up lodge at the end of the drive. We set off, trying to keep out of sight of the hall by dodging from tree to tree.

At last we reached the lodge. We headed around the back, found a little ramshackle greenhouse, and sat in there. And waited. At first it was quite exciting; we ate the pink shrimp and made lots of plans about how Fang was going to hunt down the Beast of Gargoyle Hall and get rid of the horrible Vultures. But as time went on and there was no sign of Mathilda, it began to get boring. And then, as it grew colder and drops of rain started falling through the broken glass of the greenhouse, it got very boring indeed. By now all the pink shrimp were gone and both our tummies were rumbling. It was growing dark and we were getting desperate—we were playing I Spy.

"I Spy with my little eye, something beginning with . . . *P*," said Wanda.

"I don't know," I said. "We've done all the *P*s already. We've done *pots*, we've done *potatoes* (moldy), we've done *parsley* (dead), we've done *pebbles*, we've even done *pants*—and I *know* you can't see my pants, Wanda. There aren't any more things beginning with *P*."

"Do you give up?" asked Wanda.

"I give up."

Wanda waggled one of her rabbit ears. "Pink!"

"Pink is not an object," I told her. "Pink is a description of an object. And besides, the object is not pink any longer. It is yucky gray and—ooh! I can hear a motorbike!"

We both jumped up and rushed around to the front. We saw the single light from the headlamp on Mathilda's motorbike. As it drew nearer we saw the outline of the sidecar, and sitting in the sidecar we saw the unmistakable shape of Sir Horace.

The motorbike came to a halt. It was making its usual *putt-putt-putter-putt* sound, but now it had a strange rattle, as well. I hoped there was nothing wrong with it. Fang was sitting on Sir Horace's lap with his tongue hanging out, looking very excited, but Sir Horace looked decidedly wobbly, like a pile of cups that have been stacked up too high and you just know that if you even breathe on them they will fall over. Personally, I do not think it is a good idea for five-hundred-year-old suits of armor to travel in motorbike sidecars.

Mathilda pushed up her goggles and quickly said, "Before you say anything, Araminta, Sir Horace insisted on coming. He said he could not leave a . . . oh, what was it . . . a dismal in this dress—"

"*Damsel* in *distress*, actually, Mathilda," I said.

"Yeah? Well, one of those, whatever it is, to face such danger alone. So then I had to get him

out of the house without Aunt Tabby seeing. It wasn't very easy."

I didn't imagine it was. There was no way Aunt Tabby would have allowed her favorite suit of armor to go roaring off in a motorbike sidecar. But now we had a problem. While it would be easy to sneak the ghost of a wolfhound into Gargoyle Hall, it was a completely different matter with a rusty old suit of armor that looked as though it was about to fall to bits at any moment. I now realized that it wasn't the motorbike making the odd rattling noise—it was Sir Horace. He raised a shaky armored glove and gave me a little salute.

"At your service, Miss Spookie," he boomed, and I was relieved that his voice was still as loud as ever. He pointed at the lights of Gargoyle Hall, which we could see flickering through the trees. **"Onward! We shall take them by storm and defeat the Foul and Vile Vultures."**

Mathilda revved up the bike. "Don't look so worried, Araminta!" she shouted over the engine noise. "Sir Horace has a plan! We'll see you there!" And she zoomed away down the driveway. As I watched them go I saw Edmund riding way behind her, hanging on like a limpet.

I was not pleased. As chief detective it is my job to have the plans—it is definitely not the job of a rusty five-hundred-year-old ghost. And I was not pleased to see Edmund, either, as I knew he would just get scared and be in everyone's way. But there was nothing I could do about it. Mathilda and her three ghosts were now no more than a red light bouncing along the driveway, heading toward Gargoyle Hall—with a pink rabbit following them.

"Come on, Araminta!" the rabbit yelled. "This is going to be fun!"

I knew Wanda was excited because Edmund was there, and I felt cross because Wanda is *my* sidekick. I didn't want Wanda listening to Edmund and not to me, which is what usually happens. Not that I was jealous or anything.

As we got nearer to the hall I saw something suspicious. There was a long ladder going all the way up to an attic window—a little arched window, just like the one in Matron's room.

"Look at that ladder," I whispered to Wanda. "That is very suspicious."

"Why?" Wanda asked.

"Because ladders always are. Every detective knows that."

I wanted to investigate, but we had to get to Gargoyle Hall before Mathilda barged in with Sir Horace and messed up all my plans. We arrived, completely puffed out, just in time to see the big doors close as Sir Horace, Fang, Edmund, and Mathilda disappeared inside. I was about to grab Wanda and push her up the steps to follow them, when the Vultures came marching around the corner, so I pulled Wanda back behind a column. Then I peered out to see what my two Prime Suspects were doing. I gasped.

"What is it?" whispered Wanda.

I was too shocked to reply.

The Blue Vulture was carrying Miss Gargoyle's precious school register! Now I knew what that ladder had been for. They had climbed up to Matron's room and stolen it.

I felt so cross that I jumped out from behind the column and yelled, "Hey! Give that back!"

The Yellow Vulture shrieked, but the Blue Vulture was made of tougher stuff. She laughed. "Oh, hello, weed. Decided to come back, have you? Well, you're too late, ha-ha!"

Now, every chief detective knows that when a Prime Suspect has something dangerous that you have to get hold of—like a gun or something—you have to be calm, call them by their name, and speak very slowly. So that is what I did. "Now, Vile," I said, "just give me the register. You know perfectly well that it doesn't belong to you. You know it is school property."

The Blue Vulture gave a horrible cackle and stuck her beak in my face. "Ha-ha! Like I said, weed, you're *too late*. There isn't a school anymore, so how can it have any property?" Then she ran off up the steps and into Gargoyle Hall with the Yellow Vulture close behind. As the doors swung closed, Wanda and I heard a horrible crash.

"Sir Horace!" we both said.

We found Sir Horace's armor scattered across the checkerboard floor. We could see the real ghost of Sir Horace transparent and shimmering, standing in the middle of the pile of metal. He was tall and thin, wearing a tunic and long-sleeved shirt, and he was staring down at all the bits of metal strewn around his feet. Fang was beside him, his mouth hanging open and his ghostly fangs glimmering with ghostly dog spit.

"Ghosts, Vile!" the Yellow Vulture shrieked.

The Blue Vulture didn't say anything. She just clutched the school register close to her and looked kind of shocked.

Amazingly, it was Edmund who really terrified them. Edmund did look good. He was glowing a very spooky green and floating two feet off the floor, just like a ghost should. Suddenly he began to do a proper ghostly moan. **"Oh, Sir**

Horace . . . **Oh, Sir Horace** . . ." His weedy ghostly voice echoed around the entrance hall. It was so spooky it even gave *me* goose bumps.

The Vultures were petrified. "Aaaaargh!" they both screamed.

"**Grrrrr**," growled Fang.

"**Oh . . . Sir Horace** . . ." moaned Edmund.

"Run for it, Foul!" yelled the Blue Vulture,

and they headed toward the front doors. But there was no way Chief Detective Spookie was going to let her Prime Suspects escape.

I jumped in front of them, waggled my arms, and went, "Booooo!" like a real ghost would do.

"Aaaaargh!" they screamed again. They skidded to a halt, but before I could grab the school register they were off, racing toward the big stairs that go up to the classrooms.

"I'll get them!" yelled Mathilda. She sprinted after them, but one of her little pointy shoes got caught in one of Sir Horace's big pointy feet and she went crashing to the ground. The Vultures were going up the stairs now and I knew that in a moment they would disappear into the depths of the school and we would never find them or the register again.

I headed after them but a stupid pink rabbit grabbed hold of me. "No!" it said. "I've got a much better idea."

"Let go!" I told the rabbit. But it wouldn't. It had a surprisingly tough grip for a pink rabbit.

"Edmund!" it yelled.

"**I am here . . . Wanda . . . ,**" Edmund said in his moany voice as he wafted toward us.

"Edmund. Chase those horrible girls and herd them into a closet or somewhere where they can't escape."

"**Yes . . . Wanda,**" said her faithful sidekick.

I have to admit, that was a very good plan, and I was surprised that I hadn't thought of it first. But I suppose that is why a chief detective needs a sidekick—eventually they will do something useful. I just hoped Edmund was up to the job. "Stand guard over them, Edmund," I told him. "And don't let the school register out of your sight. Do you understand?"

"**I . . . understand,**" Edmund said, and he zoomed off after the Vultures, waving his arms around and moaning in a really brilliant ghostly way. It was the best moan I have ever heard (and living with Wanda, I hear quite a few moans, I can tell you).

The Vultures turned around and saw Edmund

coming straight for them. They gave a piercing double-Vulture screech and raced off, *clickety-clackety* up the wide, sweeping stairs.

"Go, Edmund!" Wanda yelled. "Go, go, go!"

~11~
THE BEAST OF GARGOYLE HALL

The Vulture screams began to get fainter and fainter as Edmund chased them deeper into Gargoyle Hall. Then we heard a door slam and there was silence.

"He's done it!" Wanda exclaimed. "Isn't Edmund clever?"

Now, any good detective knows that you cannot rely on weedy ghosts to do what you ask them to. "I think we ought to check," I said.

"But we need to hurry," said Mathilda, hopping around, still trying to get her shoe out of Sir

Horace's foot. "It's dark now and the Beast might soon be out."

"Ooh . . . ," said Wanda.

"**Miss Spookie!**" A ghostly boom came from right beside me. I got such a shock that I nearly did a Vulture screech. It was Sir Horace, looking shockingly ghostly out of his suit of armor. "**Allow me to be of assistance. I will attend to my page.**"

"Oh, thank you, Sir Horace," I said. I knew I could trust Sir Horace to stop the Vultures escaping.

"**And for your protection, Miss Spookie, I leave you my trusty hound and my sword.**" With that, he bowed and walked away, his long, thin feet floating just above the ground. It was so different from seeing Sir Horace clanking around in his armor that it made me feel quite shivery.

Now it was time for Chief Detective Spookie to follow her hunch. My hunch—and you will be really surprised about this—was not, as Wanda thought, that the Beast of Gargoyle Hall was the Vulture's pet. It was that the Beast actually *was* the Vultures inside some kind of Beast suit. But like all detectives, I needed evidence. Evidence is what you need to prove that a suspect has done something, even if they say they haven't. I reckoned I knew just the place to find the evidence we needed—the Vultures' room. And with the Vultures out of the way, now was the perfect time to look for it.

Gargoyle Hall was a big place, but luckily Mathilda knew her way around. She led us up some dark, winding stairs with rickety banisters. Even though Sir Horace's sword was really heavy, I was glad I had it—it made me feel adventurous. Up and up we climbed with Fang following us, lighting the way with his ghostly green glow. At last we got to the floor below the attic, and Mathilda led us onto a landing just like the one at the end of our corridor, with a phone and a trunk elevator. There were lots of dark, creepy corridors leading off and Mathilda chose the darkest and the creepiest. Even when she switched on the lights it was still creepy, because the lights were not very bright and there were lots of shadows. I was glad we knew we were not going to bump into the Vultures.

Because of my hunch, I was pretty sure we were not going to bump into the Beast, either, but Wanda wasn't. She held my arm in a tight rabbit-grasp and whispered, "Suppose the Vultures' pet is missing them, Araminta? Suppose it decides to come and look for them?"

"Don't be silly, Wanda," I whispered. "The Beast is not their pet." But the spooky gloom

was getting to me and I did not feel as sure as I sounded.

The corridor had lots of little doors opening off it, which were the rooms for the senior girls. Above each one was a window, and most of the windows had pictures stuck in them—to stop people from jumping up and looking in, Mathilda said. Soon we came to a door that I knew at once belonged to the Vultures' room—it had pictures of ghouls and zombies in its window.

We stopped outside the ghoul door and listened. Fang sat down and put his head on one side, listening too. It was very quiet.

"Maybe the Beastly is asleep," whispered Wanda.

"Stop it, Wanda," I said. "The Beast is *not* asleep."

Wanda did her googly-eyed stare. "You mean it's *awake*?"

"No, I don't mean that," I hissed. But Wanda was beginning to scare me. Suppose she was right? Suppose that the Vultures did have a pet Beast? And suppose it really was inside their room, waiting for them to come back?

"Go on, then, Araminta." Wanda gave me a push.

"If you're in such a hurry, why don't *you*?"

"But you are the one with the sword, Araminta."

So I gave the sword to Wanda. "Not anymore."

"But I don't want it," said Wanda, trying to give it back to me.

"Girls!" said Mathilda. "Stop arguing. Give the sword to me, Wanda. We're going in!" With that, she pushed open the door and stepped inside, sword at the ready. Fang raced in and then Wanda and I tiptoed in after her.

"Oh no!" Wanda gasped. "The Beastly has wrecked the place."

The room was trashed. It looked like someone had gotten a huge bin of rubbish and thrown it all around. But Mathilda wasn't bothered at all. "Oh, lots of girls' rooms look like this," she said. "You two stand guard by the door and I will search."

"What do we do when you find the Beastly and it tries to escape?" Wanda asked nervously.

"You and Araminta will have to stop it," said Mathilda, edging through the piles of rubbish, poking at them with the sword, while Fang stayed right beside her like the faithful hound he was.

By now Wanda had really spooked me and I was thinking she was right—the Beast of Gargoyle Hall was the Vultures' pet. It was hiding somewhere, waiting for them to come back, and it wasn't going to like being poked by a pointy sword one bit.

"Do you think it has very big teeth, Araminta?" Wanda whispered.

"Enough, Wanda," I hissed.

We watched Mathilda poke Sir Horace's sword under the beds, stab it at the curtains and all the piles of clothes until the only place she hadn't poked the sword into was the wardrobe. And the wardrobe was, I reckoned, just the right size for a pet Beast.

But Sir Horace's sword was making Mathilda brave. She threw open the wardrobe door and jumped back. A big black furry thing fell out and

Wanda screamed. I screamed too, just a little bit, but not nearly as loudly as Wanda did.

We all stared at the pile of black fur on the floor.

"Is it dead?" Wanda whispered.

Mathilda poked it with the sword. "It was never alive."

"Oh," said Wanda, sounding disappointed. "So it's not the Beastly?"

"No." Mathilda picked up the black furry stuff and began shoving it back in the wardrobe. "It's not."

But at last Chief Detective Spookie stopped being spooked by her sidekick and remembered her hunch. "Yes it is!" I said. "*That* is the Beast of Gargoyle Hall!"

"Don't be silly, Araminta," Mathilda said grumpily. "It's just a load of fake fur."

Now, I have a Ghost Kit at home and I can recognize a Beast Kit when I see one. I waded through all the mess, got hold of the fur, and held it up. My hunch had been right all along. It was a big and furry Beast suit with four long arms, and was just the right size for two thin Vultures to fit into.

Wanda gasped. "It *is* dead! Someone's chopped its head off!"

"No they haven't," I said. I crawled into the wardrobe and began to rummage through the junk at the back. I soon found what I was looking for: a huge lumpy thing with a fat snout, big pointy ears, and fantastic long, curved teeth like tusks. I had found the head of the Beast of Gargoyle Hall! I felt around inside it and found two switches, then I pushed the head out of the wardrobe door and switched them on. It was great. The eyes shone red and an earsplitting roar echoed into the room.

"*RAAAAAAAAARRRRGH!*"

Wanda shrieked, Fang barked, and even Mathilda yelled, which was fun.

I scrambled out of the wardrobe, and while Wanda and Mathilda held up the suit, I put the head on top of it. It really did look frightening. I was impressed.

"I wonder which Vulture wore it?" said Wanda.

"I expect they took turns," said Mathilda.

But Chief Detective Spookie had worked it out. "No they didn't. They both wore it at the same time. See, it's got four arms and the head is really wide—it's a twin suit!"

"I don't know why," Mathilda said, "but that is very creepy."

She was right. It was.

I felt really pleased. Spookie's Detective Agency had done it again. It had solved the Mystery of the Beast of Gargoyle Hall.

"Now," I said, "we can take the suit to Miss Gargoyle to prove that it really was the Vultures and that the Beast of Gargoyle Hall is gone forever."

"And Miss Gargoyle can get everyone to come back to the school," Wanda said excitedly. Normally it really annoys me when Wanda finishes what I am saying, but I was so pleased that my hunch was right that I didn't mind at all. "And Araminta and I can dress up as the Beastly when we go and see Miss Gargoyle," Wanda said. "And then she can see how really, really scary it is!"

"No, Wanda. You and Araminta *cannot* dress up as the Beast," Mathilda said. "The poor woman has had enough frights for one day."

I knew Mathilda was right, but even so, it would have been fun.

We set off to see Miss Gargoyle. I carried the Beast head, Wanda had Sir Horace's sword, Mathilda took the suit, and Fang led the way. The senior girls' corridor did not look as scary as it had before, but halfway along Fang suddenly stopped and I saw the ghostly hairs on the back of his neck go up like a brush. Then he opened his mouth, threw back his head, and let out an amazingly bloodcurdling howl. **"Arrooooooooooh!"**

I felt a shiver go all over me. There is something very eerie about Fang's howl.

Wanda looked scared. "Why is Fang howling?" she whispered.

"I don't know," I said. "It's very strange. Fang

only ever howls at Uncle Drac's bats. Shush, Fang. *Shush!*"

But Fang would not shush. **"Arroooooooh!"**

"Araminta," Wanda shouted over the howl, "I can hear screaming. Can you?"

I could certainly hear something. And when I listened hard I realized that Wanda was right.

"It's the Vultures," said Wanda.

"They're coming this way," Mathilda said. "I can hear their shoes."

So could we. The *clickety-clacketies* were almost as loud as the screams now.

Wanda looked really scared. "What shall we *doooo?*"

"What's the problem?" I said. "The Vultures are finished. We know what they've been doing and we've got the Beast suit to prove it."

"But they are bigger than us," Wanda said. "And much nastier. Suppose they take the Beastly away from us. Then no one will believe us."

"There's no point risking it," Mathilda said. "We'll hide in this bathroom. Come on!" she said, pushing open a nearby door. We headed into the bathroom, but Fang wouldn't come; he just stayed in the corridor howling.

"Arrooooooooooooooooooh!"

The trouble with a ghost hound is you can't grab hold of its collar and take it with you—you have to persuade it to come. So I went outside to do that. And I wished I hadn't.

At the end of the corridor I saw the Vultures outlined against the bright lights on the landing. I couldn't see Edmund at all. But what I could see looming up behind them was the horrible shape of a massive monster. It was so tall that, as the Vultures hurtled into our corridor, it filled the entire space, right up to the ceiling.

"Oh no!" I yelled.

"What is it?" Wanda's quivery voice asked from inside the bathroom.

"It's the *real* Beast of Gargoyle Hall," I said. "And it's coming our way!"

~12~
CHIEF DETECTIVE SPOOKIE

Fang hurtled off toward the Beast, howling as he went, "**Arrooooooooooh, arrooooooooooooooooooh!**"

The Vultures skidded to a halt. They were trapped: a horrible Vulture sandwich between a slavering wolfhound ghost in front of them and the Beast of Gargoyle Hall right behind them.

"Quick!" hissed Mathilda. "Fang will keep them at bay and we can get away down the fire escape at the end of the corridor." And she headed off.

Wanda went to follow her but I grabbed her rabbit collar. "No!" I said. "Wait!"

Chief Detective Spookie had been adding up some evidence. I had been thinking about a particular page in the *Beastly Bats* book and also about what Uncle Drac had said in the van. At the sight of the real Beast, I had what detectives call a breakthrough—I suddenly realized what it was. It was the cute little blue bat that had stowed away in my trunk. It was the bat that had caused all the trouble back at home. *It was a rare and deadly Transylvanian werebat.* Wow!

"Wanda—get in the bathroom!" I yelled.

"*What?*" Wanda looked horrified.

"Please, Wanda," I said. "It's *really* important. Get in the bathroom. Close the door but *don't lock it.* Okay?"

Sometimes Wanda is a good sidekick because she does understand when there is a real emergency. And this one was real, that was for sure. "All right, Araminta," she said.

"Take the shower-snakey thingy off the bath, get the shower running really fast with cold water, and be ready to point it at the door."

"Okay." Wanda nodded. She looked really serious.

"The first person to come in will be me, then the Vultures, and then the Beast. Spray the Beast with the shower as hard as you can. Okay?"

"Okay. Can I spray the Vultures, too?"

"Beast first. Then Vultures. Ready?"

"Ready!" Wanda scooted into the bathroom and slammed the door.

I took a deep breath and headed up the corridor toward Fang, the Vultures, and the werebat. I didn't mind getting closer to the Vultures, but I did mind getting so near the werebat. It was horrible. It had huge blue furry wings with curved claws at the end of them, tiny orange eyes, and lots of very sharp, pointy teeth. It was homing in on the Vultures' hair and they had their hands on their heads, screaming, "No! No!"

I almost felt sorry for them. Almost.

Now came the scary part—I had to get the werebat to follow me. And to do that I had to get its attention, which was never going to happen with the Vultures screaming and Fang howling like a mad wolf. I remembered the word Sir Horace uses to make Fang do as he is told. "Fang," I said. "*Fidelis*. Quiet, please."

Fang stopped howling and looked at me, which was good. The Vultures stopped screaming and gawked at me, which was good. The werebat looked down at me with its piercing orange eyes. This should have been good too, because I needed to get its attention, but it didn't feel like that at all. It felt really scary.

"I'll help you," I told the Vultures. "Follow me, okay?"

"Yes, yes," they said. "We'll do anything. *Anything!*"

I set off down the corridor, waving my arms and trotting in a really silly Wanda-style way— which I hoped would make the werebat want to chase me. I glanced behind to see Fang bounding at my heels, then the Vultures following me in exactly the same Wanda-style. If I hadn't been so scared by what was following *them* I would have burst out laughing. But close behind them was the werebat, flapping its big leathery wings and making an excited high-pitched squeaking noise.

I reached the bathroom door, raced in, and there was good old Wanda standing in the bath, holding the shower spray. It was going full blast. She looked at me and for a moment I thought she was going to spray me, but she didn't. She watched me hurtle in, then Fang, then the Vultures come screaming in at top speed, and still she waited just as I had asked her to. I pushed the Vultures out of the way and as soon as the werebat was through the door, Wanda turned the shower to it and blasted it.

Splooooosh! The werebat fell to the ground with a loud *splat*. And there it stayed—a huge, soggy heap of blue leathery skin and fur lying on the bathroom floor. Wanda kept right on blasting until I said, "Okay, it's not moving. You can stop now."

Wanda grinned, then wheeled around and turned the shower on the Vultures.

"Argh!" they yelled. "Stop it! Stop it!"

Wanda is not a mean person, so she did stop it. But the Vultures were soaked through—they looked very thin and very wet, like two half-drowned cats.

"What are we going to do with them, Araminta?" Wanda said.

"We will put them in their room, where they can't cause any more trouble," I said.

"It's all right, we're going," said the Yellow Vulture.

"There's no way we want to stay *here*," said the Blue Vulture, and they dripped soggily into their room and shut the door. We heard the key turn and then there was silence.

We left Uncle Drac's werebat lying on the floor in a puddle and closed the bathroom door. When we got outside, Wanda said, "But when it dries out and feels much better, it will come looking for us."

"Wanda," I said, "it has tiny little claws at the end of its wings, which are no good at all for undoing bathroom doors. There is *no way* it is going to get out of there."

We bumped into Edmund, zigzagging along the corridor, moaning and waving his arms. **"Oh, Wanda, Wanda,"** he wailed. **"Something awful has happened!"**

"We know," I told him crossly. "You let the Vultures escape."

"Don't be mean to Edmund, Araminta," Wanda said. "He is very upset."

"Yes, Wanda, I am. I am very upset," said Edmund. "The Vultures ran right through me. They are very pointy and sharp. Oooooh!"

Even though I had now solved the Mystery of the Beast of Gargoyle Hall *and* the Spookie House Mysteries—because they were all caused by the werebat—Chief Detective Spookie knew that there were still a few last parts of the Mysteries to piece together. And here was a witness who could help her do that. "Edmund," I said. "Calm down and tell me what happened."

Edmund's voice was all trembly and squeaky. "I did what Wanda asked me to," he said. "I herded the Vulture girls into a big closet with books in it. Then Sir Horace and I kept guard. But the little blue bat with the orange eyes from Spookie House was in there, hanging upside down in the corner. And that frightened me because I know what happens to that little bat when the moon comes up."

"Ooh, Edmund. *What* happens?" asked Wanda. I sighed. I should have thought my sidekick would have worked that one out by now.

"Oh, Wanda, it is terrifying. It changes into a huge, furry monster-bat and gets very hungry. Then it looks for something to eat."

"Oh, *Edmund*," said my sidekick.

"When the moon came up that's exactly what it did. Suddenly there was a huge blue monster with orange eyes in the book closet. I think it tried to bite one of the Vulture girls."

Wanda giggled.

"It was not funny, Wanda," Edmund said. "It was horrible. They ran out screaming. They went right through me. And then the monster chased after them and that went right through me, too. It was very spiky, although not as spiky as the Vulture girls."

It was then that I remembered something very important. "Edmund," I said, "where is the school register?"

"It is in the book closet, Araminta. Sir Horace is guarding it."

"Good, that means it is safe. Now I am going to call Uncle Drac."

Wanda stared at me, puzzled. "Why are you calling Uncle Drac?"

I sighed. Wanda will never make chief detective. "Because," I told her very patiently, "it is *his* werebat. It comes from the caves where Uncle Drac went on vacation."

Wanda looked cross. "Well, you might have said that Uncle Drac told you all that."

"But Uncle Drac didn't tell me," I said. "I worked it out. So I have now solved *all* the Mysteries. I *am* chief detective, after all."

Wanda stared at me. She didn't say anything for quite some time. And then she said something really nice. "*All* of the Mysteries . . . That is very clever, Araminta. You deserve to be chief detective."

~13~
THE BONKERS BARON

Ringy-ring, ringy-ring. The phone rang in faraway Spookie House. It was late, very nearly midnight, and I guessed that everyone there had gone to bed. After an awful lot of rings I heard Aunt Tabby say, very crossly indeed, "*Yes? What do you want?*"

"Hello, Aunt Tabby," I said very politely. "It is Araminta, your niece, here. I would like to speak to Uncle Drac, please."

"Araminta!" Aunt Tabby yelled so loudly that her voice went right into the middle of my head.

"What are you *doing*? Why aren't you in *bed*? What time do you call *this*?"

"It is nearly midnight, Aunt Tabby," I said. "You really should get your clock fixed."

"Araminta, have you just called to tell me to get my clock repaired?" Aunt Tabby asked crossly.

"No, actually, Aunt Tabby, I haven't," I said very patiently. "I have telephoned to speak to Uncle Drac. Like I said."

"I don't know where he is and I am not getting out of bed and walking all around Spookie House to look for him either," said Aunt Tabby. "You will have to speak to me instead."

I knew that tone of voice. There was no way Aunt Tabby was going to get Uncle Drac to come to the phone. So I said, "Could you please tell Uncle Drac that his werebat is here at Gargoyle Hall? It stowed away in my trunk and got out. But tell him that he is not to worry because even though it has been chasing the Vultures, we have it under control now. But it would be good if he can come and get it tomorrow. Thank you very much." And I put the phone down.

Wanda was looking at me, impressed. "Wow. What did Aunt Tabby say to that?"

I shrugged. "I don't know. I gave her the message like she asked me to and then I hung up."

Wanda grinned. "I expect she is saying a lot to Uncle Drac right now," she said.

"Yes," I said. "I expect she is."

Mathilda had gone to tell Miss Gargoyle and Matron what had happened and show them the Beast suit, so we decided to go and see how she was doing. Edmund was calmer now. He floated along behind us, casting a nice ghostly green glow over everything while Fang trotted beside me. We bumped into Miss Gargoyle bouncing out of Matron's room like an excited beach ball. She gave us a really big smile. "Mathilda has told me everything. Well done, girls!" she said.

"Now you can get the school going again," I said.

"Yes, Araminta, I think we can," Miss Gargoyle said, her eyes twinkling.

Suddenly Matron called out, "There's a car coming up the driveway!"

"At this time of night?" Miss Gargoyle called back. "Whoever can it be?"

"Ermintrude." Matron sounded worried. "Ve haf trouble. Big trouble."

Miss Gargoyle hurried back into the room. I followed and found her looking out the little window. Peering over her shoulder, I saw the long beams of the headlights shining through the trees as a big, shiny black car swept up to the entrance. A driver in uniform got out and walked smartly around to the back. He opened the door and a tall, thin man in a black suit stepped out. From the window we could see the top of his shining bald head, which was fringed by long white hair. He looked just like a . . .

"Vulture!" I gasped.

"It's the Bonkers Baron," whispered Miss Gargoyle.

"Vot is he doing here?" Matron whispered back.

Miss Gargoyle looked very flustered. "I don't know. We must go down and meet him. Oh dear. Oh deary-dear." She bustled out and we all followed her. Halfway down the corridor, she stopped and her hands flew to her mouth. "The school register!" she said. "Those ghastly girls have still got it. Oh, what I am going to *doooo*?"

"It's all right, Miss Gargoyle," I said. "They don't have it anymore. Sir Horace is guarding it."

"Sir Horace?" asked Miss Gargoyle.

"He is a ghost. But he is a knight and will guard it with his life."

Miss Gargoyle gave me a headmistressy look. "A ghost has no life with which to guard anything, Araminta," she said. "Oh dear, I really *must* have that register."

"We'll go and get it right now," I said.

"Quick as you can, girls," said Miss Gargoyle. "Please bring it down to my study."

"Edmund," I said, "take us to the register."

Edmund can move very quickly when he wants to. He looked really funny. His little spindly legs were running fast, but his feet did not touch the floor. He zoomed along the maze of corridors and up and down endless stairs until Wanda and I were completely lost.

Suddenly a booming voice called out, **"Miss Spookie, where is my trusty sword?"** The eerie greenish figure of Sir Horace came hurrying out of the gloom. His ghostly hair was standing up on end—he looked like he had had a bad shock.

I felt really embarrassed—we had left his trusty sword on the bathroom floor. I guessed by now it was going rusty. And Sir Horace hates rust.

"Er. Do you need it right now, Sir Horace?" I asked.

"Yes. There are thieves and brigands at large," he said.

"I can go and get it," I offered.

"There is no time. Miss Spookie, Miss Wizzard, come at once." He beckoned us to follow him. We hurried after Sir Horace down the dark corridor. At the end was a big closet with a door thrown wide open, and as we hurried toward it the two Vultures came racing out. Clasped in the Blue Vulture's bony claws was the big red school register.

"Hey!" yelled Wanda. "You're meant to be in your room. You told us you would stay there."

They burst out laughing. "Ever heard of the word *gullible?*" the Yellow Vulture sneered.

"Yeah, ha-ha," snorted the Blue Vulture. "Gullible. And if you look it up in the dictionary, it's not there."

"Isn't it?" said Wanda.

They let out a horrible screech and ran straight at us. They ran through Sir Horace, then shoved us out of the way, their metal heels going *clickety-clackety, clickety-clackety* as they ran away cackling.

We picked ourselves off the floor and chased after them, but the Vultures knew their way through the school and we didn't. We lost them and it took us ages to get down to Miss Gargoyle's study to tell her the bad news.

When we got there, things did not look good. Mathilda was in the entrance hall putting Sir Horace's suit of armor back together. She looked really upset. "We have to get Sir Horace back in his armor," she said. "He is our only hope of stopping them from taking the school register away!"

I knew Mathilda was desperate, but I didn't think even Sir Horace in his armor could do much. "I'm going to see if we can help," I said. "There must be something we can do."

Wanda and I slipped quietly into Miss Gargoyle's study. Everyone was there.

Miss Gargoyle was standing behind her desk, looking like she wanted to cry. Matron was next to her, looking like she wanted to hit someone. The Vultures were there, looking smug. And looming over everyone was the Bonkers Baron. He was tall, thin, and beaky, just like his daughters. The way his shining bald head with its fringe of long white hair bent forward and stared down at everyone made him look so vulture-like it was almost funny. But it wasn't funny, because he had the nastiest smile I've ever seen, as though he had found something really tasty and dead to eat. He was resting one of his long white claws—I mean hands—on the school register, which lay open at the last page on Miss Gargoyle's desk.

The little clock on Miss Gargoyle's bookshelf suddenly made a whirring noise and then it began to ping. Everyone in the room stopped to listen.

It pinged twelve times. It was midnight—and a new day.

The Bonkers Baron began to speak in a flat, grating voice. "As of today this school has no pupils registered. The terms of the covenant state that on the first day with an empty school register, Gargoyle Hall becomes mine to do with as I wish."

"But that's not true," I burst out. "I am registered at the school."

"No, weed, you are not," the Blue Vulture said. "You removed *yourself* from the register. One of the conditions of being at the school is that you do not go outside the school boundaries without permission. But you did. You climbed over the fence with your rabbit friend. We saw you. And as head girls we were legally standing in for the headmistress, who was not available— seeing as she had run away screaming and locked herself in Matron's room. Ha-ha."

Miss Gargoyle sat down and put her head in her hands. It was true, and there was nothing she could say.

"But I *want* to stay at the school, so put me back on the register," I said.

"If a girl is removed from the school register for breaking the school rules, she cannot be reinstated for at least two weeks," the Yellow Vulture said smugly. "Isn't that true, Miss Gargoyle?"

Miss Gargoyle nodded bleakly.

The Blue Vulture laughed. "So that's it. There are no students at the school."

"What about me?" Wanda yelled. Everyone turned to look at her.

"*I* want to be at this school," Wanda said. "I do. I really, *really* do!"

"Well, you can't," the Bonkers Baron snapped. "Because, little girl, there isn't a school to be at anymore." Wanda looked like she wanted to kick him. She does not like being called "little girl."

Suddenly Miss Gargoyle got to her feet. "Baron," she said. "The terms of the covenant actually state that a *complete* day must pass without any students registered at the school. I am still headmistress of Gargoyle Academy for Girls and if I wish to enroll a girl at Gargoyle Academy today, then I will."

"Oh no you won't!" the Blue Vulture yelled, and she snatched the register off the desk.

"Give me the register, please, Violetta," Miss Gargoyle said.

"Don't give it to her, Vile!" the Yellow Vulture yelled.

"Of course I won't give it to her, stupid," snapped the Blue Vulture.

"Yes you will!" Wanda and I said together. We snatched the school register out of the Blue Vulture's claws, but the Bonkers Baron pounced on us. He was really strong; he pulled the register out of our hands, did a swivel on his metal heel, and *click-clacked* away. His two baby Vultures ran after him and there was a horrible crash in the hall.

We all raced out of the study to find Sir Horace's armor heaped up in a pile on the floor. Again. "Come on, Mathilda!" I yelled. "We've *got* to stop them!"

We hurtled down the steps, but the big black car's engine was running, the Bonkers Baron was already in the front seat, and the Vultures were throwing themselves into the back. There was a squeal of tires, slamming of doors, a shower of gravel sprayed into the air, and the car was gone. We stood and stared at the red lights disappearing down the driveway into the night. No one said a word.

And then suddenly, from somewhere along the driveway, there was a massive *bang*! It echoed into the night, sending the crows fluttering up from the trees, cawing in protest. There was silence. We could see headlights stopped in the distance, shining up into the trees, and we hurried off toward them—even Vultures need help if they have a car crash.

It was a long way down the drive to the headlights. Miss Gargoyle and Matron got so winded they had to stop, but Wanda, Mathilda, and I kept going. We found the Vultures' car stuck between two trees. A horrible hissing noise was coming, not from the car, but from the other side of the driveway.

Wanda grabbed my arm. "It's a snake!" she whispered. "They must have swerved to avoid a snake. Listen. It's huge!"

Even I know that huge snakes do not exist in this country. I knew at once that there must be another explanation. Besides, in the red glow of the Vultures' taillights, I saw an unmistakable outline. "Don't be silly, Wanda," I said. "It's Barry's van!"

"Dad! Dad!" Wanda yelled, and raced toward the van, which was sitting on the grass at the end of two deep tire ruts, with steam hissing out of its hood. The door opened and Uncle Drac came staggering out.

I left Mathilda to sort the Vultures out and ran to help Uncle Drac, but he was fine. "I told you," he was saying to Barry. "I *told* you. You shouldn't drive a van without headlights. But did you take any notice?"

"Well, *I* could see perfectly well, Drac," Barry said. "It's not my fault. I was blinded by those bright lights racing toward us. Far too bright, they were. And too fast. It shouldn't be allowed."

"It's your stupid van that shouldn't be allowed," retorted Uncle Drac.

Wanda and I grinned at each other. If they were arguing, they were all right.

Mathilda hurried over to us. "Does the van still go?" she asked Barry.

"Of course it does," Barry said. "It takes more than a little bump to stop a van of this quality."

"Quality!" Uncle Drac snorted.

It was then I saw that good old Mathilda had the school register! She pushed it into Uncle Drac's arms and told him, "Take this back to the school and make sure you give it to Miss Gargoyle."

Barry's van went kangaroo-hopping up the driveway, carrying its precious cargo.

I was very impressed. "Wow," I said to Mathilda, "how did you get that?"

Mathilda grinned. "The Vultures can't get out. The car is wedged between the trees. So I just reached in through the broken window and grabbed it."

The Vultures may have been stuck, but that didn't stop them from screaming some very rude words at us. We reckoned that meant they were all right too, because no one screams so many different rude words if they are not feeling perfectly okay.

Matron arrived just in time to help us push their car out from the trees. It had huge dents down each side but it still worked. It went spluttering off down the drive and we all waved it good-bye.

We were really tired, but before anyone went to bed there was something that had to be done. Back in Miss Gargoyle's study we watched as Miss Gargoyle handed Wanda a pen. "Sign here, Wanda, dear," she said.

So Wanda signed her spidery squiggle in the big red school register:

Wanda Wizzard

Miss Gargoyle gave a big smile. "Gargoyle Academy for Girls is back in business," she said.

Barry and Uncle Drac stayed the night in what Miss Gargoyle called the guest wing. The next morning Wanda and I were woken up by a knock on our room door. It was Mathilda.

"Miss Gargoyle says will you come down for breakfast, please?"

We got dressed in our school uniforms, then I picked up my little suitcase, emptied out the cheese and onion chips, and we headed off. We could smell bacon and eggs and we were both really hungry, but first there was something we had to do. We went down our twisty stairs to the floor below and headed along to the bathroom where Wanda had sprayed the werebat. There was a big puddle of water outside the door. We stopped and listened.

"Are you sure it will be tiny again?" Wanda whispered.

"Yes," I said. "The moon set ages ago. Come on, Wanda."

I pushed open the bathroom door and we padded in through the water.

"There it is!" Wanda whispered.

And there, upside down on the shower curtain, hung the smallest, cutest, shiniest blue bat ever. I very gently pulled it off the curtain and put it into my case, quickly closing the lid because I could see its little orange eyes opening and I didn't want it flying away and disappearing again. Then we set off downstairs for breakfast.

We went into the dining room and stopped dead.

"Oh!" Wanda gasped. Sitting at the table were not only Miss Gargoyle, Matron, Mathilda, Uncle Drac, and Barry, but also Aunt Tabby and Brenda (with Pusskins).

"Hello, Mom," Wanda said, sounding embarrassed. Because it is always embarrassing when your mother comes to your school, particularly if your mother is Brenda Wizzard.

"Hello, Wandy-Woo-Woo!" Brenda trilled.

Wanda went as pink as her rabbit suit had been before it got covered in spiderwebs.

Miss Gargoyle was looking at my suitcase. "Araminta, dear," she said. "Please don't pay any attention to what that awful Vulture girl said last night. You don't have to leave the school. Do please stay."

"Thank you, Miss Gargoyle," I said. "I would love to stay." I caught a surprised glance from Aunt Tabby but I ignored it. "Actually, this suitcase is for Uncle Drac. There is something in here that belongs to him." And I walked over to Uncle Drac and very carefully laid the case in front of him. Uncle Drac went to open it.

"No!" I yelled just in time. "Don't open it!"

Uncle Drac jumped in surprise. And then he understood. "Oh," he said. "Is it what I think it is?"

"If what you think it is is small and blue with little orange eyes, then yes, it *is* what you think it is," I said.

Uncle Drac broke into a huge smile, so wide that I could see his lovely pointy teeth. "Minty, you are amazing. I don't know how you did it."

"Did what?" Aunt Tabby asked suspiciously.

"Minty has just trapped the werebat. It is here, in her suitcase."

Everyone stared at my suitcase as if it were going to bite them.

"Drac," said Aunt Tabby. "I think you have an apology to make."

Uncle Drac did a little cough. "Ahem. Er. I am very sorry, Minty."

"Uncle Drac," I said, staring pointedly at Aunt Tabby, "there is no need for *you* to apologize."

"Er, yes there is," said Uncle Drac. "You see, when I was on that bat vacation, I brought back a souvenir—a very pretty little blue bat with orange eyes."

"I know," I said.

Uncle Drac sighed. "I thought it was the sweetest bat I'd ever seen. And it was so tiny, I just put it in my suitcase and no one knew. And it was fine in there. And it was fine back home, too—until it saw moonlight. And then it turned into a huge monster bat with horrible orange eyes and began eating all the baby bats in the turret. Then it moved on to the bigger ones. The more it ate, the stronger it became. My bats were terrified, which was why they kept trying to escape."

"So it wasn't my fault that they all flew out and covered Wanda?" I said, looking straight at Aunt Tabby.

"No, Minty, it wasn't," Uncle Drac agreed. "They were flying away from the werebat. And then, when I realized the werebat had escaped from the turret, I was afraid it might attack you and Wanda. That is why Aunt Tabby and I agreed with Mummy—I mean your great-aunt Emilene—to let you go away to school. I thought it was safer until I caught the blue bat."

"But you all made it seem like I was being sent away because I was bad," I said. "Which is not fair."

Uncle Drac sighed. "Life is not always fair, Minty."

Meanwhile, Wanda was looking very cross. "You didn't care about *me* being safe," she said to Brenda and Barry. "That is very unfair indeed."

"But you had Pusskins to protect you," Brenda said indignantly.

"Pusskins!" Wanda said in a disgusted voice. "Huh!"

I was still thinking about things being fair. "But it is a good thing that the werebat came here," I said. "Because it meant that the Vultures got scared by a monster just as much as they had scared everyone else with *their* monster. And that was *totally* fair."

And no one disagreed with that.

After breakfast, Miss Gargoyle gave me and Wanda the Vultures' Beast suit as a thank-you present. Then she set about calling all the girls who had left the school to tell them that the Beast of Gargoyle Hall and the Vultures had gone and were never coming back. Ever. By the end of the day, Miss Gargoyle had more than fifty girls signed up for the school. There was no way the Bonkers Baron was going to get hold of it now.

That evening, Great-aunt Emilene arrived. She came sweeping up the steps with her double-ended ferret bouncing along, gave Miss Gargoyle a hug, and said, "Ermintrude, I am *so* pleased it has all turned out well. I knew that once I managed to get Araminta here, she would sort it out. She is quite the young detective." Then, to my total amazement, my great-aunt turned to me and winked.

I was shocked.

It was then that I realized that Mysteries are mysterious things. Sometimes when you solve one Mystery, you find another one lurking underneath—a hidden Mystery that you did not suspect at all. I smiled—I had learned something really important for a chief detective to know. And I now knew the *real* answer to the Mystery of Why Chief Detective Spookie Was Sent to Boarding School. I felt really happy—until suddenly, Great-aunt Emilene said to me, "You remind me so much of myself as a girl, Araminta."

I felt a lot less happy after *that*.

Wanda looked at me and grinned. "Now I

know what to get you for your next birthday," she said. "A double-ended ferret."

"There are worse things," I told her.

"Like what?" Wanda asked.

"Like a pink rabbit suit."

But later, as we stood on the steps waving good-bye to Uncle Drac, Aunt Tabby, Brenda, Barry, and Great-aunt Emilene, I thought what fun it was to be at boarding school with Wanda.

And to be sharing—and wearing—the best Beast suit in the whole wide world.